REBEL HEART

The Harts of Texas: Book One

BARBARA MCMAHON

Rebel Heart
Copyright © 2016 Barbara McMahon
All Rights Reserved

One

Wiping her damp palms on the seat of her jeans, Shannon Blackstone tilted her chin and walked down the hospital corridor, trying for a confident and assured look. Her heart pounded in her chest, her hands curled in nervous energy. Pausing by the curtain that shielded the cubicle from the busy hustle of the emergency room, she took a deep breath. Slowly she parted the curtain and peered in.

The man lying back on the high gurney caught the slight movement and turned his head, his eyes catching sight of her standing in the opening.

"Come on in, darlin'. You looking for someone?" Jase Hart's voice was husky and low, and unexpectedly sexy.

Shannon took another breath then darted a quick glance over her shoulder to make sure no one hovered about to challenge her right to speak to the patient. Seeing the way clear, she slipped through, the curtains giving the illusion of privacy.

Even lying down, he looked big. His bare chest gleamed like bronze beneath the fluorescent lights. The light dusting of curly hair matched the color of the dark blond on his head. His muscles contracted, relaxed, rippling beneath the taut skin as he cradled his injured arm with his right hand. Dusty jeans looked out of place in the sterile environment, but eminently suited to him. The aged cowboy boots hung off the edge of the gurney, attesting to his height. To his profession.

She swallowed and stepped closer.

"I'm Shannon Blackstone, Mr. Hart. I came to see if you're all right," she said, stopping four feet away, afraid to step closer. Butterflies fluttered in her stomach. Nerves she had expected, but not the startling pull of attraction. It had been ages since she'd felt the slightest interest in any man. And she never wanted to be interested in a cowboy again. Frowning slightly, she tried to ignore the fascination that slowly burgeoned within.

"Well, sugar, you didn't have to come all the way down here. I'll be right as rain in no time. Couple of broken bones, nothing that won't mend. Who are you, the hospital welcoming committee?" he asked, his gaze traveling across her, down her, taking in every inch of slender frame.

Shannon knew he wouldn't be swept away by her looks. Clean and wholesome was as good as she got. Though, she recalled almost nostalgically, Bobby had once waxed poetic about her long black hair and smoky blue eyes. But then he'd waxed poetic about a lot of things, including bulls and broncs. She was neat, her long, dark hair pulled back into a single braid that hung down her back almost to her waist. Her Western shirt and sensible jeans were common attire for women in Texas. When she shook her head in response to his question, he sighed.

"Figured as much, dressed as you are. All the nurses here wear some kind of informal uniform," he mumbled, his eyes meeting hers again. His were silvery gray, fringed with thick, curly golden lashes that softened the hard planes and angles of his tanned face. For an instant heat flashed in his gaze, then wry amusement settled in.

Shannon's internal temperature rose at his look. She stared at him, trying to keep her eyes on his, though they longed to roam over the superb male body lying there. His shirt lay with his hat on a nearby chair and her eyes filled with the vision of his wide masculine chest. The tanned skin covered well-defined muscles. The sprinkle of golden hair tantalizingly invited her fingers to brush through, to feel their crinkly texture. His belly was hard and tight, bisected by the snug jeans he still wore. His boots were old and scuffed and dusty. He raised one knee, placing the boot on the end of the gurney.

She sucked in a deep breath. He was a handsome guy and probably knew it. But she was determined to resist any attraction. She'd had enough heartache to last her a lifetime. Cowboys were strictly off limits. Resolutely she held his gaze.

"I saw you fall," she said. "It looked bad." For one horrified moment she had been afraid he'd been killed. That would have put paid to her plans.

He smiled, amusement dancing in his gray eyes. "So you came rushing to my side to give me aid?"

"Hardly," she said dryly. She stepped nearer, watching him closely, trying to determine the extent of his injuries. He continued to cradle one arm across his chest, and he hadn't even attempted to sit up since she appeared. Did he have injuries other than the broken arm? A bruise spot high on his cheekbone discolored the even tan. Studying him warily, she asked, "How bad is it?"

"Busted arm, cracked ribs. Be right as rain in a few weeks." He dismissed it carelessly, as most of the men she knew would have done. They were so stubborn in their manly pride--unwilling to admit to any discomfort, no matter how hurt they were.

"But not soon enough to get back on the rodeo circuit this year?" she asked.

"Holds me back a bit," he acknowledged. "But won't put me out."

"Trying for the nationals?" She stalled, trying to find out more about him, trying to find a chink in the conversation to slip in her request. Slowly she wiped her damp palms against her jeans again.

"Yep, going to make it all the way this year." He was cocky, confident, and heart-stoppingly gorgeous. Which he probably used to his advantage when flirting with all the buckle bunnies who followed rodeo cowboys. She knew all about men like him. But she needed him.

"Won't being on the sidelines for a few weeks put an end to your chances?" She raised her eyebrows, not surprised at the cocky arrogance of the man. They were all alike, these rodeo cowboys, bold and brash and sure as anything that they were God's gift to the world.

"I'm high in the rankings. I just have to make sure I ride enough to get back up there when I get back into action." He frowned. "Do I know you?"

She shook her head, biting her lip as the moment arrived. She wondered at her nerve, wondered if he'd agree to her plan or laugh in her face.

"No, but you knew my husband, Bobby Blackstone."

He stared at her, startled surprise clearly etched. His eyes lost their humor as he assessed her. "I didn't know Bobby was married," he said slowly.

She shrugged. "Can't help that. He was, and to me." For a moment the old anger and bitterness threatened to overwhelm her, but she clamped down on the emotions. Her marriage had ended a long time ago. No good would come from letting the old hurt swamp her now.

"I rode some with Bobby before he died," Jase said, as if denying her claim to the marriage.

"We'd been married a year and a half when he died," she said simply.

Jase fell silent, his eyes narrowed as he studied Shannon. She didn't move a muscle. She wondered what thoughts filled his mind, but she wouldn't ask. What he thought didn't matter if only he'd listen to her request for help. She didn't know what she'd do if he refused.

"He never said he was married," he said at last.

"I'm not surprised. He didn't much act married when he rode the circuit. He mentioned you to me a lot those last months. When I heard you were competing in the events today, I thought…I mean, I came to talk to you. I need some help and I thought you might listen, being a friend of Bobby's and all. Now I wonder if maybe you'd need someplace to go while you're healing."

His lopsided smile charmed her. She stiffened at the

reaction, frowning slightly. She didn't want to like the man, only wanted to tap into his knowledge, get him to help her get back on her feet.

"So you rushed down to offer a place to stay?" he asked, his eyebrows rising.

"Sort of. Actually, I thought maybe you could help me out and I could help you out."

"Doing what, darlin'?" His eyes were dancing again, and this time his grin almost undid her. Her hands clenched tightly to resist reaching out to touch his muscular arm, to test the heat of his skin. Would he scorch her, or was his skin cool in the air-conditioned hospital? Either way, she had no business even wondering. She had come with a definite purpose!

"Um, if you can't ride for a while, maybe you need a place to stay? As it happens, I need a knowledgeable cowboy to give me some pointers on ranching. So I thought we could work a trade. Room and board in return for some instruction."

"Pointers on ranching? You planning to buy a ranch?"

"I already own one. It was Bobby's and mine. I inherited it all when he died."

"That happened over a year ago. You only looking to get some pointers now?" he asked in disbelief.

"I had a manager, Rod Thompson, but—"

The rasp of rings along the track interrupted as a tall nurse yanked back the curtains.

"Who are you?" she asked, spying Shannon.

Before she could answer, Jase answered for her. "Kissin' kin. She's come to hold my hand while you torture me, sugar," he said easily to the nurse. His wink caught Shannon by surprise. She half expected him to tell the nurse she was bothering him and ask for some privacy.

"You hardheaded cowboys don't even know the meaning of torture. The X-rays are done and the doctor's waiting to set that arm. You can come along if you're family," the nurse said, turning to Shannon. She ignored the flirtatious banter of her patient, though the slight smile conveyed she enjoyed it.

As she maneuvered the gurney from the cubicle, Jase reached out with his good arm and snatched Shannon's hand. Linking the fingers of his uninjured hand through hers, he tugged her along beside the trolley. Smiling up at her, he winked again. "I need moral support, darlin', you wouldn't want to desert me in my hour of need, now, would you? You can tell me more about why you came looking for me."

Tingling sparks of attraction danced up her arm. Her eyes widened in surprise as she hurried to keep up with the gurney. She didn't like feeling this way. She was content in her life. She had her ranch, and the prospects of making something of it, if she could only learn enough.

Jase radiated self-assurance. Did he expect women to fall over themselves to be with him? Had he misunderstood what she wanted?

The nurse was tall, with long legs and in no mood to dally with her patient. Shannon couldn't have said a word if her life depended upon it as she hurried beside him, bemused by the glittering lights in Jase's silvery eyes and by the shocking feelings coursing through her from his clasp. Of course she found him attractive, Shannon told herself, but that didn't *mean* anything. She wasn't going to give in to her feelings no matter what. She'd come here for business, not to get tangled up with some cocky rodeo cowboy, no matter how gorgeous he was, or what his smile made her feel.

Trying to yank free, she found that, injured or not, he was strong. His grasp didn't hurt, but he let her know she would be free only at his say-so, not her own. She glanced at him, but his eyes were closed, a slight smile curling his lips. They were firm and chiseled. For one shocking moment Shannon wondered what they might feel like against her own. Appalled at her thoughts, she skipped another step and concentrated on keeping up with the brisk pace set by the nurse.

The doctor quickly applied plaster to Jase's arm and, though he tried to keep from hurting his patient, Shannon knew Jase was in pain from the hard grip on her hand and the beads of sweat on his forehead. Yet he never said a word in complaint--keeping up his easy banter, flirting with the nurse, joking with the doctor. Even taking a second to check up on Shannon from time to time.

His forearm was broken in two places, two ribs cracked, and he had a slight bump on his head. The doctor treated each injury efficiently, while keeping up a steady lecture on the foolishness of rodeo riders.

"No riding until the arm's healed. Check with me before you go trying to kill yourself again," the doctor grumbled, giving the cowboy a slap on his thigh when his ribs had been wrapped.

"You know, doc, I wasn't trying to kill myself, just ride the damn horse."

Shannon shook her head in disgust. That's what they all said, pretending it wasn't dangerous. To them it was a sport, never mind the fear and heartache it brought their loved ones. That had been Bobby's favorite saying, *I'm only trying to ride the horse.*

She tried to free her hand but Jase's fingers tightened slightly and he tilted his head to see her.

"Shannon, here, will take good care of me until I'm ready to compete again, won't you, darlin'?" he asked, his eyes brimming with some secret amusement.

Did that mean Jase was going to help her out?

She turned to the doctor. "Any special care?"

"No, just no competition until he's healed. I don't envy you, young lady. These guys are never easy to deal with."

She nodded, remembering her own husband and how she'd never understood him, never understood why he'd insisted on performing, competing, flirting with other women. She clamped down once again on the emotions that threatened her. She didn't have time for them now. She could only go on, wiser now, she hoped.

"Come on, cowboy, let's get out of here. I'll drop you where you want to go."

She needed to get back on track, offer him the job and be on her way home. She didn't like rodeos or hospitals and she'd had more than enough of both today.

Ten minutes later Jase and Shannon stood by her truck in the back parking lot of the hospital. He wore the shirt he'd competed in, torn, dusty, one sleeve gone, very much the worse for wear. It didn't detract from his masculinity. On the contrary, it seemed to enhance it even more.

Shannon kept her gaze averted, feeling safer that way. All she wanted to do was get back on the road and head for home. She wanted him to come to the Bar Seven with her. She needed someone she could trust. And Bobby had spoken highly of Jase from the first. Would he help her for Bobby's sake?

"You want to tell me a little more about these pointers you want?" he asked, leaning against the side. He tilted his hat down until it shaded his face, shadowing his eyes. The pristine-white sling looked out of place against the dusty clothes, it seemed insubstantial against the broad chest and shoulders. Shannon hadn't realized how tall he was until they'd left the hospital. He towered over her own slight frame.

"It's simple. I want to learn to run the ranch myself. I had a manager, but he snuck out a couple of weeks ago, taking all the ready cash in my account. I'm not going to make that mistake again," Shannon said firmly. "I want to learn everything so I can run the place myself. I've had to learn the hard way that men can't be trusted."

He leaned toward her at that comment.

"Whoa, now, honey. One man steals some money and you come to the conclusion all men aren't to be trusted?"

"Oh, no, Jase, Rod Thompson wasn't the only one to hammer home that lesson. Bobby Blackstone started the whole process. Rod only completed it." She met his eyes, hers flashing.

His hand came up to brush across her cheek, tuck an errant strand of hair behind her ear. "I thought Bobby was your husband."

"He had trouble remembering that," she said bitterly.

Bobby hadn't been able to stay away from women, even after marrying her. She'd been a fool, blinded by love, a mistake she'd never make again. She ducked her head away from his hand.

"Then he was an idiot," he said in his slow drawl.

Before she could say anything to that startling comment, he continued. "So you want to learn to run a ranch, in exchange for my room and board for a few weeks?"

She nodded.

"Why me?"

"Bobby might not have been the best of husbands, but he seemed to be a good judge of others. He admired you, said you were the best."

He chuckled. "The doubt in your tone leads me to think you aren't too sure of his judgment."

"Well, you have to admit, anyone who would deliberately risk his life day after day riding wild broncs and bulls just for the hell of it might give a rational person a moment of doubt," she said primly.

He laughed, a rich, contagious laugh that had her smiling reluctantly, sharing the humor.

"It's wild and free and like nothing else in the world," he explained.

"Wild and free, like you? Don't you think about

settling down and getting on with your life?" she couldn't resist asking.

Bobby'd tried. For several months he'd tried, but had not been able to resist the lure of the rodeo circuit. The fast life, fast women and thrills drew him like an addiction. Shannon, who had never understood it, had only, finally, accepted it. Would they still be married and sort of happy had Bobby lived? Would he ever have tired of the challenge?

Stunned by the swiftness of the change in Jase at her comment, she watched helplessly as his eyes grew stormy, his face grew remote and austere. For a second, Shannon felt a brush of fear. What had she said?

"I've had enough responsibility to last me a lifetime. Now I'm doing what I want for a while, and that's rodeoing. If you have a problem with that, maybe I'm not the man you're looking for." For a moment, the hard lines of his face were ferocious.

Her heart banged in her chest. She longed to step back, put some distance between them, but she planted her feet, tilted her chin and remained where she was. She'd obviously touched a raw nerve, but she wouldn't be cowed by the man. She needed him, and fate had provided her something to offer in return, a place for him to recuperate.

"What you do with your life is your own business. But you need to stay somewhere while you heal. I only want your help while you can give it. I'm not asking for a long commitment. Just until you're healed and ready to move on, why not help me in exchange for room and board?"

"You came to the rodeo today to see me. Do you have second sight? Did you know I was going to take a fall and bust my arm? What were you going to do if I hadn't had the accident?" He leaned back against the truck again, lines of pain and fatigue bracketing his mouth.

"I planned to ask for a recommendation from you. I know you know ranching, Bobby mentioned it more than once. I thought you might recommend someone honest to help me. When I found out that you were hurt, the other idea came to me. It's perfect. You'll have a place to recover, and help me out at the same time."

He stared down at the pavement for a long moment then nodded. "Yeah, it has a certain appeal. You think you can learn everything that fast? This arm'll heal in about six weeks, then I'm back on the circuit, with a lot of lost time to make up."

"I can learn some things in six weeks. It would be a start. Then maybe you can recommend someone else. What have you got to lose? You need a place to stay, don't you?"

He started to say something, then stopped. Shrugging his shoulders, he winced as the pain tore through his arm and chest. "Yeah, I guess I could use a place to stay. You've got yourself a deal, Shannon Blackstone." His hand reached for hers and he shook it gently. He then turned and opened the door on the passenger side of her truck.

"I need to go back to the arena so I can get my truck and horses."

Jase tried to ride the bumps in the road as Shannon

drove back to the fairgrounds. The doctor had offered some pain meds, but he needed to stay sharp until his horses were taken care of. He didn't know if the bump on the head when he fell was clouding his judgment, or if the decision to help out temporarily was a good one.

He glanced at the woman beside him. He needed to check out her story. Had she really been married to Bobby Blackstone? He remembered the cowboy. They competed sometimes in the same event. Bobby had been good. And wild. And one of the biggest flirts on the circuit.

Shannon was pretty in a quiet, wholesome way. Not like the flashy gals that hung around rodeos looking for a good time.

It wasn't long before they reached the fair grounds. He directed her to the back where the rigs were parked. His horse had been taken care of by someone, he could tell. The gelding was hitched to the side of the trailer, with plenty of water in a portable trough.

"Are you able to haul the trailer?" he asked. It wasn't like driving a car.

"Sure. I've done it plenty of times. But how do I get my truck home?"

Despite refusing the drugs, he was having trouble concentrating. His arm ached. Breathing hurt. And the truck could use some new shocks. He was sure they'd hit every bump and pothole on the drive from the hospital. Now he had to come up with a way to get her to drive his rig to her place. Probably not a good idea to suggest she leave it here for six weeks.

"Oh, I can't believe it, it's Steve Sturney and his son

Petey."

Before he could even ask who they were, she was out of the truck and almost running after two cowboys sauntering along beside the horse trailers.

Two hours later Shannon drove Jase's big truck, hauling the double horse trailer behind them. Jase dozed in the passenger seat. She still could hardly believe she'd run into a neighbor and his sons at the fairgrounds. Petey had agreed to drive her own truck back to the Bar Seven. Jase had given his keys to Shannon, clearly doubting her ability to pull the trailer. But by the time they'd cleared town, he'd seen she was fully capable of handling the rig and he relaxed.

She glanced over at him and felt a tug at her heart. He looked much younger sleeping against the door. His long lashes brushed against his tanned cheek, the lines caused by pain eased with the medicine he finally took when he was assured she could handle the rig on the drive to the ranch. His position looked uncomfortable, but he was oblivious to all discomfort as he slept.

She concentrated on the road. It'd never do to become too interested in Jase Hart. She had one purpose--learn all she could about ranching so she'd never be taken in by a swindler like Rod Thompson again. The ranch was all she had. She had to make a go of it. It'd been an unexpected legacy from Bobby and the only thing of value she'd ever owned.

She had picked up some skills after she and Bobby had married. But her background didn't include ranching. She'd been the only child of an Air Force pilot. Her mother had died when she'd been a baby. A tornado when she'd been in high school had leveled her home and killed her father. She'd barely made it through high school after that.

Luck had given her a good job at a local bank. Several years of experience had her applying and being accepted for a junior management position at the bank in Tumbleweed where she'd met Bobby Blackstone.

The ride to the ranch took more than an hour. She drove carefully, conscious of her passenger and the magnificent cutting horse she pulled. She wanted to give both of them the most comfortable ride possible.

When she turned off onto the gravel drive that led to the house, she glanced once again at Jase. He was awake, watching her.

"Feeling better?" she asked as the gravel crunched beneath the tires. The grassy hills rolled out before them crisscrossed with barbed wire fencing. Cattle were visible in the distance. She loved this part of Texas. The hills were beautiful in all their moods and she never wanted to live anywhere else.

"So this is your place?" he asked, looking around as they drove further into the ranch.

"Yes." Pride echoed in her voice. She smiled as she gazed over the spread. She'd learn everything she could to run it properly. She wanted it to be a showplace.

"Some of it's deeded land. Some of it's leased from BLM, Bureau of Land Management."

"I know the BLM, darlin'," he muttered, amused. "What do you run?"

"Polled Herefords." She threw him a dark glance. "My name's Shannon."

"I know, you told me."

"I'm not your darling," she said stiffly.

He chuckled. "Early days yet, darlin'."

"This is strictly a business arrangement, Jase Hart. I'm not at all interested in anything personal."

"Now, darlin', that's a bigger challenge than trying to teach you to run a ranch. Don't be throwing out statements like that or you might find yourself up against more than you bargained for," he said, amusement lacing his tone. His voice was disturbingly husky.

She closed her eyes briefly as his voice washed through her. She tried to concentrate on driving the truck.

Despite the attraction she felt, she knew better than to get involved with a cowboy. Never again. Tilting her chin, she pulled into the yard, drove past the ranch house and to the big barn behind it. She cut the engine and turned to glare at him.

"I married a cowboy, I know all about how charming you all can be, and how you have the faithfulness of a rutting stag. All I want from you is your help in teaching me enough to run the ranch efficiently. Save the rest of your flirtatious ways for a woman who wants them."

He studied her then nodded. "As you say, darlin'."

He opened the door and stepped out.

Save it for someone who would believe in it, as she once had. And as she longed to again. At the unbidden thought, she pushed open her door and hurried to the rear of the horse trailer.

"I'll get your horse out," she said, swiftly opening the ramp and letting it down.

"I can manage," Jase said, wincing as he watched the ramp reach the ground.

"Are you always so stubborn?" she asked. She scrambled into the trailer and moved to the horse's head, soothing him with easy words of praise as she located his lead rope and snapped it onto the halter.

"Do you always rush in where someone else could do it?" he asked from the back.

She grinned, peeking around the big gelding, and nodded. "Always." Slowly she backed out the gleaming horse.

"He's a beauty," she said as she drew level with Jase. Standing on the ramp, eye level with him, she wished that she could always be that tall. With a sigh she continued down until he towered over her again.

"Shadow. He's a champion."

"Champion cutting horse?"

"That's right." Jase reached out and took the lead line from her and headed toward the barn. Shannon kept up with him.

"I thought you rode the broncs."

"I do. I also participate in the cutting events. Shadow's won me a ton of money. We should do even better this year. And I can ride him when I can't ride the broncs."

"You need to make sure your ribs heal, not just your arm." Why was she telling him how to run his life? He was all grown up. It didn't matter to her if he healed before he headed out. She only wanted his knowledge to help her on the ranch.

"I'll stay the six weeks. Don't worry about that."

"He can have this stall." She swung open the door to the stall, watched as Jase settled the chestnut in the large box stall, then opened the door on the far wall that led to the corral. "He must be worth a lot if he's winning you prize money."

Jase shrugged. "I don't want to sell, so I don't know what he's worth."

"If you sold him you'd have some ready cash, maybe enough to buy a place of your own," she said slowly.

He closed the door, latched it, leaning on the top bar to watch the horse explore his new home. "I don't need the money to get a place. What I want to do is ride the circuit, see some of the country, be responsible to no one but myself. Go where I want, when I want, do what I want."

She turned away, surprised at the shock of hurt that plunged through her. Those had been Bobby's feelings. Even though he professed to love her, he'd wanted to leave and do his own thing. The responsibility of the ranch had proved too much. The responsibility of being married had proved too much. She hadn't asked to fall in love with her husband. She'd wanted a man to love, someone she could depend on to be there for her, someone she could build a life with, not have visit when the mood struck.

"Where do I sleep?" Jase asked as she gazed at the gelding.

She blinked, the thought of him in bed flooding

through her mind. Feeling the steal of color in her cheeks, she desperately hoped he couldn't read minds.

"You can have one of the extra bedrooms in the house." She swung around and headed swiftly for the house.

Jase grabbed his duffel bag from the back of the truck as they passed and followed her, his boots crunching the gravel beneath his feet, ringing hollow on the wooden porch.

"Down here." She didn't pause when she entered the house, but headed down the hall to the large guest room on the left, several doors from her own. It would do.

The house had been built for a family. She'd once hoped she and Bobby would fill it with lots of children. Now she lived in it alone.

She stepped aside so he could enter, watching him fill the room with his presence. For a moment, she wondered if she'd lost her mind. Why have him stay in the house? Rod had had a room in the bunkhouse. Was she crazy to put Jase so close? She was only fooling herself if she thought he'd need any help because of a mere broken arm. Putting him so close was like putting a torch near a keg of gunpowder. She'd better watch her step, or it was all likely to blow up in her face.

"This'll do fine," Jase said as he surveyed the room. Then he turned to her, staring at her for a long moment. He took a step closer. His eyes were smoky gray. His lips were lifted in that easy half smile of his. The injuries faded into insignificance beside his blatant masculinity.

Shannon's pulse sped up, her breathing became more difficult. Was he going to touch her? Kiss her?

Heat suffused her body. She knew she should turn, should walk away, but she was paralyzed, like a deer in headlights, unable to move, unable to reason, only capable of feeling.

To her utter surprise, he closed the door in her face!

Jase turned and swept his hat off and tossed it on the dresser. Gingerly removing the sling, he shrugged out of his shirt. He hoped he could get his boots off, but if not, he'd sleep in them. He was about out for the count as it was. Five minutes later he'd fallen into bed, pulled the coverlet over his chest. He ached everywhere. And he couldn't for the life of himself figure out why he agreed to Shannon Blackstone's crazy idea of him teaching her to run a ranch profitably.

The last thing he wanted was to be responsible for anyone other than himself. And some starry-eyed young woman would be a bigger responsibility than he'd ever known if he let her.

Two

"Morning, darlin'," Jase's lazy voice called across the kitchen.

Shannon paused, then turned, the fork still in her hand. Momentarily she forgot the bacon she was cooking as she took in the tall, rangy cowboy leaning casually against the doorjamb. His voice traced through her senses like hot syrup, warm and sweet. His easy grin and devilish eyes touched her with a lazy sensuality that was disturbing and totally unwelcome.

She scowled and nodded to the table.

"Have a seat. I was going to bring your breakfast to your room. I didn't know if you'd be up and around today or not. You took a hard fall." She turned back to the sizzling bacon. She was beginning to doubt whether her plan, which had seemed so practical in theory, was going to work. How could she get anything done, learn anything to help her become a better rancher when she was so very aware of Jase as a man?

"No need to wait on me, darlin'. I'm not your responsibility. It'll take more than yesterday's knock to slow me down."

"Stop calling me darling. And while you're on this

ranch you sure are my responsibility. Just as all the hands are. How do you feel today?" She tried to get on the offensive and take charge.

"Better than yesterday, worse than tomorrow." He drew back a chair, scraping the floor. Shannon jumped at the sound, throwing him an angry glance. It was a mistake. His eyes caught hers, the silvery shimmer held her mesmerized.

He was the one that broke first, trailing his eyes insolently down her small frame, taking in the loose cotton shirt, her snug jeans, the scruffy boots. Slowly he traced back up and met her gaze again; his, clearly hot and interested.

It made her blood boil—especially when she could feel the heat rise at his gaze. She tilted her chin, masking her churning emotions with disdain, and turned back to the stove. Her hand shook slightly, but she knew he couldn't see. Scooping up the last of the bacon, she didn't even bother with any effort with the eggs, she scrambled them all.

Five minutes later she set the heaping plates on the table. That had proved to be the longest five minutes in her life. She'd felt his gaze bore into her back every second. She knew he studied every move she made, and was a hairbreadth away from making some annoying comment. And if he had even hinted at anything—

A darting glance at his face let her know he knew she'd have blasted him to kingdom come if he'd opened his mouth. And Bobby had liked the man! She shook her head. She'd always thought her husband had had some smarts, now she wondered.

"You always put your foreman up in the house?" Jase asked as he tucked into the hearty breakfast.

"I thought you might need something during the night. When you're well, you can move out to the bunkhouse."

"Hardly worth it. I won't be here that long," he said easily. "You're a good cook." He had almost finished the meal.

"Thanks for saying it, but it doesn't take much to cook eggs and bacon."

"These biscuits are light as air."

They were good, and one thing she excelled in. Actually, Shannon could cook. She could do a lot of things, but not run a ranch. Yet.

"You didn't grow up around here?" Jase asked as he poured himself another cup of black coffee and tipped back in his chair. His cast on his chest, he rested his cup against the plaster. He studied his hostess.

"No, farther west in a podunk town you've probably never heard of."

"That where you met Bobby?"

She shook her head. "We met in Tumbleweed, soon after I transferred here with the bank."

Her reply was short. She didn't want to discuss her past. She wanted to get on with learning all she could before he moved on.

"Why not go back?"

She looked up at that. "There's nothing to go back to. This is my home, and the only means I have of making money. I have to learn how to run it profitably."

"What do your folks say to your staying here all

alone?"

"First of all, I'm not alone. Gary and Dink are in the bunkhouse. Second, I don't have any folks. Both, my parents are dead." She scraped back her chair and picked up the empty plates. "Don't you worry about me, Jase Hart, I'm my own person, not your responsibility. From what I see, you don't cotton to responsibility at all."

"You don't think rodeoing is a responsible way to make a living, I take it." Amused by her attack rather than annoyed, he baited her. Taking another sip of the coffee, he waited for her response.

She hesitated a moment. She hardly knew the man, she had no business insulting him—she needed him. But she longed to wipe that smirk from his face. He made her mad, or was she still mad at Bobby?

"Do you think riding wild horses for eight seconds is a responsible way to make a living?" she asked, her sudden anger frightening her.

The amusement faded from his gaze and he tipped down his chair. Resting his good arm on the table, he leaned forward and stared at her. "What's the real message here? I'm not responsible enough for you? If I had a spread somewhere and was working on it, I wouldn't be here helping you out. Which do you want, Shannon?"

"I need your help."

"And even my lack of responsibility must be overlooked to get the help you want, right?"

She nodded. "You seem old enough to settle down, maybe get started in something that will provide for you in your old age. Rodeoing is a dangerous sport. Witness yourself right now. How much longer can you keep getting your bones broken and your ribs cracked? It's a young man's sport."

"Some of it is, the broncs and the bulls. But team roping and cutting events can be done until a man's eighty. I'm not all *that* old, dammit. I'm not ready to hang up my spurs."

"You started late, didn't you? I remember a little of what Bobby said when he talked about you."

"I turned pro late, but I've competed since I was a kid." Shutters came down, his expression grew remote.

Shannon blinked at the change. This man before her now wasn't the carefree laughing man she'd faced only moments ago. He looked hard and mean and dangerous. Yet there seemed to be a hint of bleakness in the depths of his gray eyes. What had she said to change him?

"You let me take responsibility for myself. You have this ranch. You learn to run it and I'll be out of your hair. I sure don't need anything or anyone complicating my life at this point. I've worked too hard to get free," he said.

He stood abruptly. "I'm going to check my horse. When you finish the dishes, come out and you can show me around the place."

"I'll do exactly that, but only because that's what I planned to do, not because you're ordering me around." Shannon glared at him, afraid to give an inch lest he take over.

The amusement flashed back in his eyes. "While I'm here, I run this ranch. I'll teach you everything I can. It's up to you to learn as much as you can as fast as you can.

But while I'm here I make the decisions and what I say goes."

"Wait a minute, mister. This place is mine and I'm not relinquishing control of it to anyone!" She stepped closer, ready to go toe-to-toe with him. How dare he think he could just waltz in here and take over.

"There can be only one teacher, one student, and in this kind of business the only way to learn is by example. If you know so much, maybe you don't need me, Half Pint," he challenged.

She stopped only a foot away. "Let's get one thing straight, no one makes comments about my size."

He chuckled and reached out a hand to tilt her face up toward his. The feel of his fingers against her skin shocked her. Heat spread like lightning through her. Her legs grew weak and Shannon wondered if they would continue to hold her upright. Tingling sensations spiraled from her jaw to her heart. Her gaze caught in his, she could feel the heat of his steely gray eyes warm her. She forgot the discussion, forgot the indignation she'd felt only moments before. She forgot everything except the sexy man standing before her, holding her jaw so she had no choice but to stare into his mesmerizing silvery eyes.

"Shannon." His voice was low and husky. "I'm not insulting you for your size. You're dainty and petite and pretty as a rose in full bloom. But you're awfully small to be struggling with a ranch of your own. A lot of the work is hard physical labor. Hard for a full-size man. What do you think you can do? You can't weigh one hundred pounds soaking wet. I weigh double that and am at least a foot taller. Honey, to me you are a half pint."

"I make up for size in determination," she said. She was resolved to make it in this man's world without depending on anyone. She just needed some help to get going.

He smiled and brushed his thumb across her jaw, slowly, back and forth. His callused skin slightly abraded the softness of hers. Taking a shaky breath, Shannon breathed in his unique scent: spicy, tangy, masculine.

Shannon's hand came to cover his wrist; she had to break contact between them before she did something foolish beyond belief—like throw herself into his arms. But when she felt his strength, the warmth of his taut skin, her fingers clung. She could feel the steady beat of his pulse beneath her fingertips, feel the leashed strength of his muscles as he gently brushed his thumb against her. When he rubbed across her lips, she trembled. Opening her mouth slightly, she drew in a deep breath. He was going to seduce her right here in the kitchen!

Yanking back, she turned, her determination rising. She refused to become emotionally caught up with some no-account cowboy who wanted freedom from responsibilities of building a future.

"Call me Shannon." She cleared her throat, trying for a stronger tone. "I'm not your darling, nor honey, nor a half pint."

He laughed and headed for the door.

"You know better than that, darlin'. Hurry out and we'll ride the range."

"You can't. The doctor said no riding till your ribs healed."

"He meant bronc riding." Jase filled the doorway, his cocky stance brash and fresh. Except for the cast and the slight discoloration on his cheek, he looked fit and trim and raring to go.

"He meant until you got well," she gritted from between clenched teeth. "I didn't bring you here to damage your well-being further."

"Right. We both know you want my expertise to help you come up to speed in running this place."

She nodded, hesitated a moment. "You can, can't you? Teach me what I need to know?"

He shook his head, amazement and amusement warring for supremacy. "You're asking that now? Maybe you should have asked that before you invited me to your bed and board."

"Not my bed," she protested. Her heart raced at the image that flashed, both of them together in the big bed she'd bought a year ago. She slammed her fist against the table. She would not daydream about Jase Hart!

"An expression only." His grin threatened to split his face.

"Bobby said you were the best all-around cowboy he knew, and a man could learn a lot from you," she said slowly, getting her emotions under control. Running her hands down her jeans, she tried to soothe her jangled nerves. She felt as if she were on a roller coaster ride, thrilled, scared, anticipating the next dip or crest.

"Yeah, well I can ride and rope. And just to set your mind at rest, I grew up on a ranch in the eastern part of the state. I ran it after my folks died, made enough to get my younger brother and sister through college. So I think I can handle this place for a few weeks. But I meant what I said, Shannon. I'm the boss while I'm here. I'll teach you everything I can, but you take my orders around the place like everyone else. When I leave, you're on your own."

She wanted to protest, to wipe that smug look off his face. But she merely nodded once, clenching her fists tightly. She didn't know enough to kick him out. But as soon as she did, he'd be gone so fast his head would spin.

"Concerning the ranch, you're the boss, while you're here," she agreed.

"So meet me in the barn in half an hour."

"But concerning everything else, I'm the boss," she said with steely determination. "And that means watching out for the health and welfare of everyone on the ranch. We're not riding today!"

"Damnation! You are the most stubborn woman I've ever met." He glared at her.

"Well you haven't seen anything yet!"

They were in a standoff, both highly charged and ready to do battle. Suddenly Shannon relaxed. She stepped back and gathered the dishes. "There's a ton of paperwork. Rod left things in a total mess. I would appreciate your help in reconciling the accounts, showing me exactly where I stand and what I can do to get through this time. I don't have any money, less than two hundred dollars in the bank. I had to let most of the hands go and I know Gary and Dink would leave if they thought they could get work elsewhere."

He paused. "I didn't realize the full extent of the

situation. Okay, let me check on Shadow then I'll be back to go over the paperwork with you. You can show me the ranch tomorrow."

She nodded, hiding her elation he'd been so easily sidetracked.

"But don't think I don't know what you're doing," he said smoothly.

Giving him a cheeky grin, she tossed her head. "So what, if it works?"

"I don't need a mother hen. I've been taking care of myself for years," Jase said slowly, his eyes burning into hers.

"I'm not a mother hen, but even I know if you do too much before you're ready you'll have a relapse and then who would have to nurse you? I don't have time for that."

"I'll meet you in the office in thirty minutes."

Jase walked quickly to the barn. He didn't know whether to swear about the woman he'd just left, or admire the way she stood up to him. Glancing around, he noted the barn seemed to be in good shape. The area around the house looked well kept. The house itself was sturdy. Large for a single person, but of course she and Bobby had the place together. Maybe they'd planned on a big family.

She didn't know how lucky she was not to have children in the mix. What if Bobby had died and she'd had a bunch of kids to take care of.

Shadow greeted him with a soft nicker when he reached the stall. Someone had already fed the horse, Jase could tell by the remnants of hay in the trough.

"Hey, boy, you settling in okay?" He rubbed between his eyes and noted the stall had also been cleaned. He had to meet those cowboys who could do the chores without prompting. Shannon might have lost money with the theft of the ranch manger, but she obviously had some good men working for her.

He walked around the barn, noting the fresh hay in the loft, the cleaned empty stalls. Through one of the open doors, he saw several horses milling around in a corral behind the barn. He wandered outside and around to the back to study the horses. There were six. Two came right up to the fence and stared at him. He patted them and softly called to the others. Slowly they ambled over. They looked like good, sturdy stock.

Returning to the house, he noted the bunkhouse a few hundred yards from the barn. That's where he should be staying. Maybe he'd move in later today.

Not that staying with that feisty woman gave her any ideas of settling him down. He smiled in remembrance. She could barely tolerate him. Man, she argued about everything.

Yet, he provoked her. He knew it. Why, just to see her eyes flash and the color rise in her cheeks?

It was a mistake. Shannon knew that ten minutes into the session. She couldn't concentrate on the ranch's books and records, she was too intensively conscious of Jase sitting only inches away. She could see his every gesture from the corner of her eye. While she was supposed to be tallying the latest count of cattle from the different sections of range, all Shannon could do was watch his fingers dance across the calculator as he figured the feed usage for the last year.

She threw down her pencil and stood up, anxious to put some distance between them.

"Now what?" he asked, glancing up.

"I need the calculator. I can't add all these numbers." She'd always been great at math, but now she found it impossible to add two plus two in such close proximity.

"I'll be finished with it in a minute." He looked back down to the feed receipts and continued his analysis. "I can't believe you don't have a computer to handle all this. I didn't know anyone still kept paper records."

"Well, now you do," she snapped. She had suggested one to Bobby when they'd first been married. She used computer equipment all the time at the bank. But he'd said no. This way no one could hack into their records.

She had wondered if he had any knowledge about computers, but hadn't argued.

Now that things had turned out the way they had, she could see why Rod didn't want one either.

Maybe now would be the time to get one.

"Do you know how to set up accounts?" she asked.

Jase nodded, concentrating on the calculations.

Shannon wandered over to the window and gazed out across her ranch. A fierce pride surged through her as she looked at the grass all golden brown in the late summer sun, the endless acres that comprised her home and livelihood. She had to keep it. It represented all she had in the world, all that defined her now. She was a rancher. She never wanted to return to working for someone else. She wanted to make this small cattle ranch the best one in West Texas, maybe even the whole state.

And to do so she needed to rely on herself alone. She refused to let herself return to the position Rod had found her in: alone, bewildered, scared. She'd learn everything there was to know about ranching and make sure she did everything right.

Turning swiftly, she walked back to the desk and sat down. Attraction or not, she had to settle down to business. Clamping down on her awareness, she leaned over Jase's arm and studied the figures he jotted down.

"Explain to me what you're doing and why. You're supposed to be teaching me things, not doing them for me."

He sat back in his chair and looked at her. Almost absently he reached out his hand and ran it along the single braid down her back, his fingers tracing the plaits, toying with the soft ends that hung free below the elastic band.

"You can graze your beef from late spring through the early fall. But for the cattle you keep over the winter months, you have to bring in feed. I'm seeing how much you used the last few years. We can get an average and know how much to expect for the coming winter. You'll need to see if you can grow your own hay in some of the fields to supplement what you buy. It's cheaper."

She listened to the words, enjoying the richness of his voice as it poured through her. He could probably read the cattleman's journal to her and she'd find it entrancing. But the feel of his hand in her hair had her mesmerized. Every quivering nerve in her body focused on his hand. Over and over he trailed his hand over her hair as he talked. Yet he looked at her, not at his fingers. How could he know what he was saying when he was driving her crazy?

She jumped, her eyes moving to his. She'd missed the last thing he'd said.

"What?"

His hand stilled in her hair as he watched her with an intensity that shook her.

"I asked you what Bobby's plans had been." His eyes narrowed as he watched her, considering.

"He didn't have any plans. He only bought this place that year he made so much money. He wanted it as somewhere to come back to. His real love was the rodeo, only I didn't know that at the time." The hint of bitterness escaped, despite her best efforts to hide it.

"So he left you behind."

"Yes." She tried a smile, but it was shaky at best. "I was an encumbrance."

"So why did he marry you?"

She swallowed, wanting to look away, unable to do so. "I often suspected because he couldn't get me any other way."

Jase remained silent for a long time as he thought about what she'd revealed. Then he spoke carefully, as if cautiously testing the words.

"A lot of women who hang around rodeos are only too willing to offer anything a man wants."

She nodded. "I know. But I wasn't one of them. I didn't meet him at the rodeo, but at the bank. He found me different I guess, from the women he was used to."

"Shy, quiet, in awe of the brash cowboys?" Jase guessed, his own eyes dropping to her lips.

She shivered as if he'd touched her. Nodding, she longed to end this discussion. It would cause nothing but heartache. She didn't want to remember, she only wanted to make a future for herself.

"I can understand the appeal. You appear almost virginal even now. I suspect Bobby's the only man you've slept with."

Shannon froze. She didn't want to discuss this, she wanted to learn about her ranch. When his hand slipped beneath her hair and cupped the nape of her neck, she leaned back, shying away from contact.

"Easy, honey, I'm not the bad guy here. I should have suspected something like that yesterday when you didn't want to hold my hand."

"I didn't, you grabbed my hand."

He smiled and nodded. "See my point?"

Shannon tried to relax. She wanted to appear at ease around him, not wired up so much she thought she'd explode. But it was impossible. He was too sexy and appealing. And she suspected he knew it, too.

"We need to clear the air, darlin'. I've thought all along you're not the type for a one-night stand. Although if you invite me to your bed, I'll give you all I have for as long as I stay here. But, honey, I'm only here for a few weeks. I had enough commitment when I was a kid. I'm taking these next few years for myself and nobody else. I'm not staying. If we make love, you need to know up front that there's no happy ever after."

She blinked, tried to draw in a shaky breath. Her

heart raced at the thought of making love with Jase. She shocked herself with a flare of desire. She'd known all along Jase would stay only until he recovered. She was lucky he agreed to help her out. She wouldn't be fool enough to set herself up for heartache.

"I can't have a one-night stand, or even a short affair," she whispered. "I'm not that kind of person." She wouldn't relax lifetime standards for a craving she'd never before experienced. He'd committed to stay for only a few weeks. She could control any wanton urges that long, surely.

He nodded, his fingers slowly drawing her closer. "I know you're not. What you deserve is a man who would run your ranch for you and offer you undying love. A man who would give you a dozen kids and come home every night, not some fool rodeo cowboy who wants to see as much of the world as he can from between the ears of a horse. But, darlin', if you ever ease up on those scruples and want a quick fling, you hunt me up, promise?"

His mouth covered hers.

His lips were warm and compelling. They moved against hers slowly, expertly and seductively, bringing her achingly aware of every fiber of her being. She longed to get closer. As if he read her mind, he pulled her into his lap, the hard cast bumping her for a moment, as he put it awkwardly around her.

Shannon didn't even notice, she was too inflamed with the sensations coursing through her, rippling through every nerve ending. Heat built, starting low and spreading to her fingertips and toes. Her breathing became erratic, but the delight that fed her from his kiss overrode every discomfort, every other sensation.

Endlessly his kiss went on and on. Shannon returned pressure for pressure, stroke for stroke, taste for taste. And reveled in it. Slowly his words resurfaced and she eased back in his arms. He released her mouth, hugging her close before setting her on his knees. She could feel the strength in his thighs, feel the leased energy that banked down the desire that rode high in him. Touched at his restraint, against her better judgment she longed for more, but took him at his word. He could not give her what she wanted most.

"I can't give you a one-night stand," she said almost regretfully.

"I know, darlin'. Best to get the urge out of the way."

She blinked. Her urges were higher than ever now—were his gone?

"And did it work?" she asked.

"Hell, no! I want you more than ever. But I'm not here for good."

She slipped off his legs, brushing her fingertips across her swollen lips. "We need to keep this on a businesslike footing, Jase. I know you are here temporarily. This ranch means a lot to me, I don't want to jeopardize it."

"I'm not putting you in jeopardy."

"No, you're going to help me save it." She sat back in her chair and looked pointedly at the stacks of feed receipts he'd been working on. "Tell me more about growing my own hay so I can reduce that feed bill. And if you have any ideas where I can get some cash, sell some steers or rent out some grazing land, or anything, let me know."

"You could get a loan from the bank."

"Beyond the bare mortgage I have, I don't owe any money, and don't want to start if I can help it. Rod really hurt the place taking all the ready cash. He didn't even pay the last round of bills, but kept that money, too. I had a little saved, but it's all gone. I don't want to get deeper in debt. What would happen if I had a bad year? I could lose everything."

"Then let's get back to work on what you have and see where you can get a few extra bucks."

That was the sensible thing to do. Heavens, she'd only met the man yesterday, she had no business wanting anything beyond her ranch. But for once Shannon didn't feel very sensible.

Three

By neither word nor action did Jase allude to their kiss. But Shannon could not so easily dismiss it. Her body still thrummed with longing as she sat beside him soaking up everything he had to say.

She couldn't believe that she'd been such a pushover, practically melting in his arms as he kissed her.

She did her best to ignore the kiss behind a cloak of interest and aloofness. She asked intelligent questions, remembering the answers. She discussed the different aspects of ranching as he brought them up. In some areas she was confident she knew how to handle things. In others she was helplessly lost.

Jase remained patient throughout the morning, though as the time passed Shannon suspected from the way he shifted in his chair that his ribs ached more than he let on.

She called a break at lunch. When he protested, she reminded him that while he might run the ranch, she was in charge of meals and rest periods and she needed to stop before her brain turned to mush. She knew better than to suggest he should rest. He wasn't the type to admit to any need, even though in obvious pain.

"Time to hit the books again," he said, after their light lunch.

"Not for me." Shannon improvised rapidly as she washed the last of the plates. "I have a few things to do first. Can we wait until later?"

"How much later?" he asked suspiciously.

She handed him the bottle of pain pills she'd brought from his room earlier and shrugged.

"What are these for?" he asked.

"You're obviously in some pain. The lines around your mouth give it away. Take one, for heaven's sake."

"Pills make me sleepy." He pushed the bottle away.

"So lie down for a few minutes. I should only be an hour. We can get back to your slave driving then," she said carelessly, turning to wipe the dishes. She smiled softly when she saw him take one of the tablets. If he'd only lie down for a while, it would do him a world of good. But try to get him to believe that. She'd taken his measure already. Macho cowboy.

In fact, Shannon drew herself up as she dried the last cup, she felt as if she'd known Jase for ages. How odd when there was so much about him that was still a mystery to her.

She couldn't explain her feelings around him. They ran the gambit. She usually took a long time to feel at ease around strangers. But once she'd gotten over being so nervous asking for his help, she had felt as if she'd known him forever. Maybe because he reminded her of Bobby a little. That same reckless endangerment of their own lives. The live-for-the-moment way they followed the rodeo.

Not that it explained her reaction to his devastating kiss. She grew weak and warm just thinking about it. Gripping the counter, she glanced over her shoulder at him. His eyes were on her. Was he remembering their kiss, as well? She refused to look away first.

"I'll lie down for a while. Come get me when you're through with whatever you have to do," Jase said, rising and walking stiffly from the kitchen.

He suspected she didn't have anything to do that couldn't wait. But it wouldn't hurt to lie down for a few minutes, let the pain meds do their thing. His arm ached, his ribs throbbed. Not that he'd admit that to anyone. Especially Half-Pint.

When he sat on the edge of the bed and fell back, he almost groaned in relief. Even with his feet still on the floor, it felt like heaven. He wasn't sure he had energy enough to get fully on the bed. He'd try it in a minute.

As he relaxed, he thought about the kiss. He'd risked a lot. But temptation had been too much. She was the most kissable woman he'd known. And he'd love to have a hot affair with her while he was on the ranch. But he'd known even before she'd confirmed it that she wasn't the type. She was love and marriage and fifty-year anniversaries. It was written all over her.

But he wouldn't mind another kiss. Or two. Before he left. Nothing more.

He was mad clear through. Shannon giggled as she heard his door slam behind her after she'd gone to wake him up. She'd let him sleep all afternoon, only going in to wake him for dinner. When he realized the time, he swore. Prudently Shannon had quickly left. Now she clearly heard the clump of his feet stomping when he got out of bed. Scooting away from his door, Shannon hurried into the kitchen, laughter spilling out. Time Mr. Hart learned he didn't get his own way in everything, acting ranch boss or not.

"What the blazes did you think you were doing, letting me sleep all afternoon?" he roared, following her into the kitchen. The savory aroma from the beef stew that had simmered all afternoon filled the air; biscuits were browning, an apple pie cooled on a rack. Cinnamon, spices, bread, all combined to bring a mouth-watering fragrance that defined her kitchen.

Jase was oblivious. He glared at her, rumpled sheet marks still visible on his cheek. Shannon ignored his anger and pointed to his chair. "Sit. Next time, Mr. Boss Man, don't be in such an all-fired hurry to get well. The doctor said it would be a while before your ribs mended. The strapping you have is to ease the discomfort, not miraculously mend the cracks. And your broken arm could use the rest, too."

"I can take care of myself."

"Yeah, right. Do you want to eat or yell at me?"

He crossed the room, his eyes narrowed, anger still simmering just below the surface. Crowding her against the counter, he stopped only inches away. The sling had been discarded, his shirt strained across the cast, across broad shoulders and his muscular chest. The glint in his silvery eyes would have frightened a brave man, but it didn't frighten Shannon.

It drove her crazy, but didn't frighten her. She held her own, meeting his gaze with hers, locking her eyes with his as the rest of the room gradually dimmed from view.

"I told you before, I don't need a nursemaid," he growled, leaning over until his nose almost touched hers.

"What do you need?" she asked softly, so softly he could scarcely hear. Her breath fanned across his cheek and a muscle jerked by his jaw.

"You, darlin'." He closed the distance and covered her lips with his. They were still warmed with sleep, grew hot as he pressed them against hers, moving persuasively, coaxingly, until Shannon could resist no longer and softened her own to meet his. Soon she was in his arms, feeling the hard length of his body press against hers. He bent her slightly over the edge of the counter as his kiss went on and on.

Pushing against him, striving for air, she was disappointed when he released her. Disappointed with herself for having given in to him again.

"Jase, please, don't. We said we would only do business," she protested, her fingers curling around the muscles of his arm, belying her rejection.

He lifted his head slightly, his eyes delving deep into hers. "We agreed I'd boss the ranch. What was this afternoon but rank insubordination?"

She smiled. "You need to rest. Your own macho image wouldn't have allowed you to admit that. It's no big deal. Sit down and eat dinner. There's time. I don't have to learn everything the first day."

She leaned against the counter for another moment,

garnering enough strength to dish up their plates and rescue the biscuits from the oven.

"If you want to learn everything about ranching, it's in your best interest if I don't sleep the day away," Jase said as she placed his dish before him.

"A few hours' rest won't set us back. Every scrap of information you give me is that much more than I knew before. Each time I think of Rod Thompson stealing my money I could scream."

"Don't let it get to you. From some of the things I saw this morning, he was clever. He probably would have been able to fool Bobby," Jase said. "Especially since Bobby was gone as much as he was."

Mollified slightly, Shannon nodded and ate quietly. She had a million questions, but most of them centered on the man sitting opposite her, not on her ranch.

She found her dinner tasteless, it was an effort to eat. She was confused at the feelings that tumbled around inside. Exquisitely aware of every move he made, Shannon had a hard time sitting in her chair. She simultaneously wanted to move closer and to run away from him. Escape alone to the outdoors, yet draw nearer and have him talk to her in his hot, husky voice. She toyed with her food, wishing the evening gone so she could seek the safety of her bed.

"Not hungry?" Jase asked, his eyes taking in her plate.

She shrugged. "Not a lot."

"It's good. A man misses home-cooked meals on the road. I usually eat at some cafe in whatever town I'm in."

"Not the stands at the rodeo?"

"That food'll kill you."

She smiled. "Thought cowboys could eat anything, something about a cast-iron stomach?"

"I like to think I'm discriminating in my tastes."

From the look he gave her, Shannon knew he wasn't talking only about food. She rose quickly. She wasn't used to the innuendos and blatant sexual looks he constantly gave.

She knew about men like him, like her husband. The chase was everything. Once a woman was conquered, it was on to new challenges. She'd guard her heart from making that mistake again.

"I have chores to do." She stalked out of the kitchen to the yard. She'd feed the horses, check in with the men and avoid temptation in the form of Jase Hart for the rest of the night.

Only she'd not counted on Jase. He came after her.

"I don't need any help," she grumbled ungratefully. Couldn't the man tell she was trying to get away from him? Avoid him?

"I need to check Shadow."

"I can feed him."

"So can I." He fell into step beside her, matching her furious pace. The familiar smile tilted his lips as he watched her stride along.

"In a temper?" he asked silkily.

"I have work to do." She wouldn't give him the satisfaction of thinking he disturbed her.

"Evening, Miz Shannon." An older man touched the brim of his hat as she entered the barn. He sat in an old camp chair near one of the empty stalls, cleaning reins.

"Evening Dink. This is Jase Hart. He's come to help out for a few weeks."

"Pleasure." Dink nodded, his eyes narrowed as he studied the younger man standing so cocky in the middle of the walkway.

"Dink," Jase acknowledged.

"Fed the stock already, Miz Shannon," Dink said easily, leaning back to resume soaping the soft leather.

"Oh? Jase's horse, as well?"

"Yep. Fine piece of hoss flesh that one."

"You should see him work," Jase said.

"I'd like to. When you going to be feeling up to riding?" Dink asked, a quick eye to the cast.

"Tomorrow."

"No!" Shannon protested. "There's more work in the office. It'll be a while—"

"I'll ride before you're up. We'll have plenty of time in the office, don't worry."

"But—"

"Lighten up, Shannon. I'm a big boy now, I can take care of myself."

She bit her lip and turned away, heading to the corral to see to her horses. She had a dozen more than she needed with only herself, Dink and Gary. But when she could afford it, she'd be hiring cowboys again and would need all these horses plus more.

If she could ever afford it.

There was still so much to do, and where was she going to get the money?

"Why did you keep Dink on?" Jase asked as he joined her by the rail.

"What do you mean?" She turned slightly to face him, her hands on her hips. "He's a good man."

"A bit old to be your number one man. Or is Gary that?"

"Dink's been here for years. He worked here when Bobby and I first bought the place."

"Darlin', he probably worked here before you were born, but that doesn't make him the best choice for your money. You'd have done better to keep one of the younger hands."

"He's been here forever and at his age he would have had the devil of a time getting work anywhere else. I feel a responsibility to him. That's something I'm sure you'd never understand!"

She was tired of fighting everything. She knew she was in danger of losing the ranch, knew she should have some young men who could do more of the physical tasks around the place, but she couldn't afford it.

And she did feel responsible for Dink and Gary. This was their home, too.

Jase wound her braid around his hand and pulled her head back until she faced him. Anger radiated from him. "Listen here, Half Pint, I'm tired of your sniping at me at every instance you get about responsibility and your belief I can't handle it. Hell, I've had more responsibility than you can ever imagine. My folks died when I was seventeen. I had a younger brother and sister to take care of. I was *responsible* for them. I barely finished high school, there was too much to do to provide a home for my siblings so the state didn't step in and send them to foster care. I've given up college and the chance long ago to enjoy the last of my teen years to provide for two other people who mean the world to me. I slaved on that damned ranch to make a living for us, to send them to school, get them started on their own lives. Now I'm taking a couple of years out for me. If that makes me irresponsible, then I admit it. But I know all about responsibility and don't want you shoving that in my face again, do I make myself clear?" His voice sliced through her like a knife.

Had his grip on her hair permitted a nod, Shannon would have done so. Since it didn't she said softly, "Yes, that's clear. I'm sorry. I didn't know."

Her eyes were wide and soft as the echo of his story rumbled in her mind. She had judged him solely on appearances. Maybe his happy-go-lucky, macho-cowboy image was only that, an image. Maybe Jase was a man who knew more about responsibility than most rodeo riders.

"So no more cracks?" His anger faded as the tight grip on her hair changed, eased.

"No more cracks," she whispered. If she ever needed reassurance that he was the man to help her, he'd just given it to her. Who would know better how to bring a ranch around than someone who had run one for years, who had made a ranch pay enough to send his younger siblings to college?

Her heart ached for the bleak picture his words painted. She longed to learn more, find out how he'd managed, what help he had had. Where were his brother and sister now? Did they still have a place on that ranch or had he left it behind to ride the circuit?

Before she could ask, however, she became aware of his fingers pulling off the elastic band that held her braid, threading through the plaits, releasing her hair.

"Don't," she said softly, her heart thudding in her chest. It was too intimate, they had to keep to a business arrangement. She needed the distance.

"Your hair is so soft," he said, ignoring her protest. "Like fine silk or soft, baby duck down." Combing through the soft tresses with his fingers, he rubbed a strand between his forefinger and thumb, let it slip through. Again and again he threaded his fingers through, letting the soft, dark hair cascade across his palm, slip through his fingers. Slowly Jase brought his head closer, until his breath mingled with hers, softly wafted across her cheeks.

"It's as soft as your lips," he whispered, touching his to hers lightly. He moved back and forth, barely touching her, the light caress as potent as the kiss they'd shared in the office.

Shannon began to shiver in anticipation. *Business, business, business* echoed in her mind as her mouth opened to his sweet assault. While intellectually she knew there was no future between them, her body craved his touch like a rose craved the sun's. Just for a moment she'd give in to the craving, then resist. One last kiss, just for a moment.

The kiss deepened and Jase braced them against the fence, his mouth roamed over hers, then left her warm, swollen lips to trace tiny kisses across her satiny cheeks, along her eyelids, to bury against her neck and trail hot kisses to the pulse point of her throat.

"You, darlin', pack more kick than a Brahma bull," Jase said against her skin. "I thought we were going to keep this businesslike."

"We are." She pushed back, hoping desperately that her gaze didn't look as starry-eyed as she felt. Her blood raced through her, her breathing came hard and fast. She tested her knees to make sure they'd hold her before pulling out of his embrace.

"We are," she repeated, trying to convince herself.

"Yeah, I can see that." He grinned at her. "Want to go riding?"

"No! And you're not going, either. Someone has to think of your ribs. If you won't, I will."

"I'll be fine. Sitting up on Shadow's no more dangerous than sitting in the chair in your office. Probably a sight more comfortable. Relax, Shannon. I won't ride tonight. But tomorrow, I'm riding out. You can come with me or let me find things on my own."

"All right, bossy. I'll go," she said petulantly.

He chuckled, rubbing his knuckles across her chin. "You stick that out all the time. What are you trying to prove?"

"Nothing."

"That's right, Half Pint, you don't have anything to prove." He put his arm around her shoulders and turned them toward the ranch house.

Shannon walked along, seething. Her hair swirled around her, unconfined in the evening breeze. His hand was heavy on her shoulder, sending tingling shafts of electricity surging throughout her. Walking wasn't easy as they moved together, his steps made smaller to match hers.

"Jase, you have to stop touching me all the time," she said once she thought she could control her voice. "I'm not some doll for you to play with."

"I never thought you were. We're business partners, right?"

"Yes, but that doesn't include touching." She tried to make her voice firm, certain.

"Don't you like my touch?"

"Yes…no!"

That was the whole problem. She did like his touch. She more than liked it. He drove her crazy with yearnings she'd thought long ago buried. She had standards that were important to her and he tried her at every turn. He had to stop!

"I like touching you. I like it when you touch me," he said slowly, the words seeping through her like a soft caress.

"But it can't go anywhere," she said softly.

"So we enjoy what we can. Lighten up, Shannon. It's only kisses."

Only kisses. She felt every one to her toes. She almost melted in a puddle whenever he was around. She'd only known him for two days, for goodness sake. What was the matter with her? She was an adult. She could handle it.

He pulled open the door to the kitchen and ushered her in.

"I'll be in the office. There are more of those feed invoices to verify. Once that's done, we'll get an accurate tally and be ready to start making some plans." The quick change from teasing to business was startling. Shannon envied him the ability.

"I'll do the dishes and then come in."

"If you want. But I can manage on my own if you have something else to do."

She nodded, glad for the reprieve. She needed to spend some time alone, get herself under control lest she throw caution to the wind and give in to his blandishments.

"Then I'll see you at breakfast," she said, refusing to meet his eyes. She could only stand so much in one night. Maybe tomorrow things would settle back to normal.

Shannon heard the jingle of spurs outside while she was flipping hotcakes the next morning. Glancing out the window she saw Jase heading for the house. When had he gotten up?

"Morning," he said, stepping inside.

"Take those spurs off. I don't want this floor marked," she commented, flipping another hotcake. She hadn't heard him this morning.

"Yes, ma'am." He grinned at her and tiptoed to the table. Sitting carefully, he removed the spurs, rising to put them by the door.

"You're up early." She turned back to the hotcakes, her heart beating double time. He looked gorgeous. His hair was slightly tousled when he took off his hat, the blue shirt that stretched across his broad chest gave a smoky tinge to his eyes. His faded jeans molded his thighs and hips like a longtime lover. She kept her eyes resolutely on the pan, afraid of where her thoughts were leading. Men should not be allowed out in public looking like that. It made a woman's concentration extremely difficult.

"Enough?" she asked as she handed him a plate piled high with pancakes. She put a platter of sausage in the center of the table and turned to get the coffee.

"Enough to start," he mumbled, already pouring syrup over the stack.

"You'll get fat." It gave her an excuse to trail her eyes over him. There wasn't an ounce of spare flesh anywhere. He had a long long way to go to get fat. For an instant she remembered his hard chest as she'd seen it in the hospital. When her eyes came back up to him, she flushed at the daring in his gaze. His smile caused her to lose her breath, he was so masculine!

"What got you up so early?" Shannon asked as she sat opposite him and began eating her much smaller stack.

"Just checking on the horses we're riding this morning. I wanted to make sure they were fed well before we left. Shadow's ready to ride, getting antsy just standing around in the corral. I work him most days to keep him in top condition."

"He's a good cutting horse, is he?"

"He's got the potential to be a great one."

"Oh? I didn't see you compete that event at the rodeo. I arrived shortly before the bronc riding event."

"We won," Jase said simply.

"Is that normal?"

"Yep. He's one of the best cutting horses I've ever seen, a natural at it. But I have to keep working him. He's the one that's been making the big money so far. Using him, I hope to make the finals this year, go on to Las Vegas to compete for best all around."

"Ambitious at the best of times. Bobby never came close, yet he thought he did all right in the standings."

"Yeah, well, I want to go all the way."

"Hard to do if you're out six weeks."

"When I'm ready to go again, I'll enter twice as many rodeos as before, that way I can increase my points fast enough to have a shot at the finals."

"As long as you're good."

"Oh, darlin', I'm good."

Shannon stared at him, the double meaning sinking in. She knew he'd be good at anything he did, including loving a woman. Blinking, she dragged her eyes away. She thought she had herself under control today.

"So we ride after breakfast?" she asked.

"Yes."

"And your ribs?"

"When they start to hurt, we'll come back." He dismissed her concern.

"What do you want to see?"

"Where the main body of the herd is, some of the range, the watering holes, where you think the best place to grow hay would be, things like that. We probably won't see everything today, but I want to see as much as we can to start."

The morning was beautiful. The sky a clear azure blue, no clouds in the vast dome. The grass was drying, the rain had been scarce lately. But it was good grazing, the kind to build meat on beef cattle. The main herd wasn't too far from the homestead and they reached the rise that overlooked the range less than a half hour after they left the barn.

Jase drew rein and sat, surveying the polled Herefords that grazed placidly before him. The herd was large, the cattle healthy and plump. Slowly he counted the steers, took in the grass available and the limitless water from the river that edged part of the property.

"You've got a good setup here," he commented as they urged the horses closer. He wanted to see some of the calves up close.

"We were lucky. The man who owned this before had no family. When he died, the state just sold it at a very reasonable price. And it was a year Bobby had done well. With his winnings and insurance money I had left from my folk's passing, we were able to buy it."

"Now you need to hold on to it. You've got a fine spread, Shannon. You can parlay it into a great one."

She flushed with pleasure at his assessment. She trusted Jase in business matters. And she was determined to hold on to her ranch, make it profitable, expand when she could, keeping her reputation growing even after Jase left.

Would he come back from time to time to check up on her? She'd like that. She'd like to see him again, beyond their six weeks together.

Or once gone, would he forget all about her? Forget about teaching her how to run a ranch and move on with his life as a rodeo rider? He'd had enough responsibility thrust upon him with raising his younger brother and sister, she totally understood his reluctance to have any further long-term responsibility toward anyone or anything.

She was on her own. Once he taught her how to run the ranch, he'd have no further need to keep in contact.

Suddenly the sun seemed dimmer. Some of the beauty went out of the day. She was struggling to learn about cattle, about growing hay, marketing techniques, and long-range planning for a long and lonely future. The ranch was all she had.

Maybe someday down the road she'd look for a mate again. But she'd make sure she chose someone more stable than Bobby had been. More stable than any rodeo cowboy looking for a good time could be.

She wanted a husband who would be home nights. She wanted someone to love, who would love her, who wanted to share the ranch with her. Someone whose kisses would excite her, whose love would warm her through the rest of her life.

How she wished that someone could look and be exactly like Jase Hart.

Four

Jase spent the next several days studying the range and Shannon's cattle. He spent hours with Dink and Gary, learning how the original owner had managed the spread, how Bobby Blackstone and then Rod Thompson had handled things.

Each morning he rode out early, getting a feel for the place, ignoring the injuries that had sidelined him from the rodeo circuit. Shannon accompanied him again the second day, but on the third, she remained home to work on the books and records. There wasn't much she could contribute to the rides. Gary knew all the answers to Jase's questions better than she did.

Jase already knew more about cattle than she. Her time was better spent gaining knowledge of her business from the records side.

Afternoons, Jase worked with Shadow, practicing cutting techniques, in the corral or out in the range with the cattle. He was tireless. The honed skill of the horse and rider were obtained only after endless hours of practice and he was faithful to that end.

Shannon watched on occasion, fascinated as the horse and rider seemed one being, working flawlessly with one another to achieve the fluid perfection. No wonder he won competitions with Shadow, they were terrific together.

Jase continued to heal. Except for an occasional catch in his breath if he moved suddenly, Shannon wouldn't have known he was still pained by his bruised and cracked ribs. She didn't know if his arm ached as it healed, he never complained and she never again mentioned he should slow down. If he wanted to push himself, it was his concern.

She had enough trouble trying to keep the interaction between them on a business footing. He was the most annoying man. Every time he came close to her, he touched her. A light caress on her arm, a brush of fingers against her cheek, a gentle tug on her braid. It was as if he couldn't keep his hands away from her. Something she was not used to. Neither her father nor her husband had been overtly affectionate.

She wanted Jase to stop. Not because she disliked it, but because she liked it too much. With the other stressful events present in her life, she didn't need his constant attentions stirring her up.

After dinner on the third evening, she escaped to feed the horses, glad for a respite from Jase. Being around him had her senses spinning. She didn't know whether to slap him down, dodge out of reach, or just endure the touching until he got tired of his little game and left her alone. She desperately needed some time alone to keep things in perspective.

She forked down the hay into the corral then spread it for the horses who jostled her, trying for a mouthful.

Putting grain in the trough, she watched to make sure Bugle didn't hog all of it from the less aggressive horses. The routine of the chores soothed her, brought her ragged senses under control.

"Did you already feed Shadow?" Jase asked, materializing beside her at the corral fence. The late afternoon sun was slowly sinking, its waning rays bathing everything in soft golden light.

She jumped, startled. "Yes. And gave him grain. I fed him in his stall so he wouldn't have to share with these guys."

Afraid to look at him, she watched the horses eat, content in the constant activity of the ranch. It had a timelessness, a continuity that she cherished. It was so different from her life before.

"We need to talk about the ranch, Shannon," he said, resting one boot on the bottom rail, resting his arm against his bent leg, staring down at her.

"We've been talking about it since you got here. What specifically?" She wanted to step away, being so near him was disturbing. But she held her ground, watched the horses, conscious of Jase's steady gaze.

"You have a mortgage payment coming soon, ranch hands to feed and pay, and some horses needing to be re-shod."

"I know." Fear clutched her. She knew all this. She'd been worrying about it for weeks, ever since Rod had vanished with her money. Where would she get the necessary funds? "I guess I have to sell some cattle, don't I? Liquidate some assets, so to speak?"

"It's a bad time for it. If you sell now you'll sell at a

loss."

"But at least I'll get some ready cash to tide me over." Damn Rod Thompson and his thieving heart!

"True." He hesitated, watching her intently as if trying to gauge her reaction. "There are other ways to get money."

She turned then to face him, anger spilling. "I told you before I don't want to borrow. The mortgage is bad enough. I can't encumber the place with more debt. Maybe I should try for a job in Tumbleweed."

"What do you plan to do, work all day then come back here and work all night to keep the place going? I don't think so."

"No one set you up as my boss. I only asked for help on learning about ranching, not on how to run my life."

"Yeah? Well the first thing to learn about ranching is that it's a full-time, hard-as-hell job. To do it right doesn't give you any time for anything else, much less a full-time job elsewhere."

"I—"

His hand cupped her chin, his thumb covered her lips, stopping the words that would have spilled out.

"And I wasn't talking about a loan. I think you could use an influx of capital. I'm offering to buy in as a partner."

She stared at him, dumbfounded. He wanted to buy into her ranch? To become her partner? Was he crazy?

Or did he think she was?

She twisted her face away from his grasp. "You're nuts. Why would I sell part of my ranch to anyone? If I can just get by this temporary bind, I'll make it."

"In the meantime this temporary bind could set you back so far you'll never dig out. Listen, Shannon. I know a lot more about running a cattle ranch than you'll learn in six years, much less six weeks. I was born on one, raised on one, ran it for a long while. I've lived, slept and breathed beef cattle until I have probably forgotten more than you know right now."

"But I can learn!"

"Sure you can, but in time to save this place? You're in a crisis situation here, sweetheart. You don't have the luxury of unlimited time to dither around and wait for the pot at the end of the rainbow. You have to get some cash and fast."

"So I'll sell some cattle. But I'm not selling my ranch."

"I didn't say sell the ranch. I want to buy in. I have some money sitting in a bank, why not help you out on the Bar Seven?"

"No. I'm not interested."

She turned and headed back to the house. Fear grew with each step. Big words, refusing his help. What was she going to do? She knew she needed a lot of money and soon. If she sold cattle now, she'd have a smaller herd, which would take longer to build up. But to sell part of the ranch, to no longer own it totally, was unthinkable. She especially did not want to give up part ownership to a disturbing cowboy who was only staying temporarily.

His arm unexpectedly spun her around. He held on to her as he leaned over, his nose almost touching hers.

She could feel the heat of his anger.

"You don't have much choice."

"I do, too. I can sell what cattle I need to raise the money."

"Why not take a partner? Shannon, I'm not asking for controlling interest, just a few shares."

"No."

"Why the hell not?" He was getting angry at her refusal and she glared up at him.

"I'll tell you why not, cowboy. First of all, this ranch is *all mine*. It is the only real home I've had since I was fifteen. It means too much to me to give up a portion of it to some stranger I only met a week ago. Second, I am not going to become dependent on another man as long as I live. I tried that with Bobby and ended up burned badly. Third—"

"Third be damned. I'm not your husband so stop comparing me to him. I'm not trying to boot you out of your home, only help you save it."

"No."

He took a deep breath, held it a moment before releasing it in a gust. "God, but you are the most headstrong woman I've ever met."

She shrugged her shoulders, trying to release her arm from his grip. But he held on.

"Why is this the first real home you've ever had?" he asked.

"I don't see what that has to do with anything," she said petulantly. She wanted to go into the house, put some distance between them. The sun had sunk behind the mountain peaks and twilight spread over the land.

The soft evening breeze teased her cheeks and Jase's proximity sent spiraling tendrils of awareness through her.

"I'm curious."

"My mom died when I was little. My dad was killed in a tornado when I was fifteen. For three years I was in foster care. Then kicked out. Do you know how hard it is for foster kids to make it?" she explained briefly in a clipped voice. She didn't like thinking back. She wanted her future to be so much better.

"And Bobby promised stability and a home."

She shrugged. He had, but the promise had proved false. Her eyes dropped to the top button of Jase's shirt, unable to continue to meet his piercing gaze. "Home is important to me," she said softly.

"And to me. Why do you think I worked so hard to provide one for my brother and sister? I wouldn't take your home from you, darlin'," he said gently. "I want to help you save it."

She shook her head. "I'm not selling."

"Fine." He straightened and released her. Stepping around her, he headed for the kitchen door.

"Are you leaving?" she asked, suddenly afraid he would do just that. Had she made him that mad?

"No." He continued inside.

Shannon followed, wondering what she was going to do next. She had so little time to come up with the money. Selling some of her cattle was the only way.

Jase sat behind her desk, rummaging around the papers stacked on its surface.

"What are you doing?" She paused in the doorway,

watching him. Would he continue to teach her about ranching? Or had she made him too angry?

"I'm trying to figure how much money you need for the next few months so we can calculate how many head of cattle you have to sell," he said as easily as if the confrontation in the yard had never taken place.

She slowly sank into the chair beside him and watched as he studied the tally sheets, ran a list of numbers on the old calculator. The mortgage payments she recognized and the salaries for Dink and Gary. There were other figures, but she was afraid to question exactly what they represented. The total was staggering.

She swallowed hard. "How much of the herd do I have to sell?"

"Don't know. Tomorrow we'll call around and find out what the going rate for cattle is right now. This is the amount you need. Once we have the rate, we'll see how many head of cattle that is."

"And then how long before I would get the money?"

"Oh, you can have it tomorrow," he said easily.

"Tomorrow?" She blinked, puzzled. How would they even find a buyer that quickly, much less get the funds?

He nodded. Tipping back in the chair, his eyes narrowed slightly as he watched her.

"Wouldn't we have to find a buyer first?"

"I'm buying."

She stared at him in surprise. "No."

He chuckled, running his knuckles down her soft cheek. "Now you're saying who can and cannot buy your cattle? Do you want to sell them or not?"

"No. I mean, yes, I want to sell, but you can't buy them. What would you do with a bunch of cattle? Are you planning to take them on the rodeo with you?"

"No, I'm planning to lease some land from you so they can continue to graze. That will generate some income for you."

"You can't do that."

"Why not?"

"You just can't."

She was stunned. She didn't know why he couldn't, but she didn't want such a close tie. Jase was only here for another five weeks. She didn't want him bailing her out of her problems. She wanted him to show her how to work them out on her own, then leave.

He had to leave before she began thinking things she had no business thinking.

"What's the alternative? Sell to someone else who will take them away. Then you lose the lease income. You've plenty of good pasture land, more than enough to support the cattle you're running. My owning some of the herd won't change that. And, in the meantime, you'll have a few months of lease income as well as the cash you need right now."

It made sense. If it were anyone but Jase she'd jump at the opportunity. Only, somehow, she felt funny accepting it from Jase.

Yet he was right, what choice did she have?

"If you buy them, it'll be at a discount," she said.

"What?"

"That way I can pay you a little bit more for helping me out."

"That's about the dumbest thing I've ever heard. You'll never make a businesswoman that way."

"I feel responsible—"

"You have an overactive sense of responsibility," he interrupted.

"It's better than having no sense at all," she retorted.

"And that's the second dumbest thing I've heard you say since we started living together."

She blinked, heat stung her cheeks. "We're not living together!"

"Oh, yes, we are, darlin', in every way but sharing a bed. I can hear you shower in the morning. Watch you cooking when I come in from checking the horses. See you in good moods and bad. Watch as you rub your eyes when you're tired and ready for bed at night."

He tilted the chair back down on all four legs and leaned toward her until his breath caressed her cheeks.

"I hear your clothes rustle as you undress each night, hear your bed sigh when you crawl into it. There's not much about living with you I don't know."

Shannon stared into his smoky gray eyes as if she were drowning. He was right. She could say the same about him. She heard him across the hall morning and night, heard the shower when he bathed. She'd wondered how he managed with his cast, his bandages. She had longed to offer assistance, but had refrained, knowing it would be the most foolish thing she could do.

She knew a lot about him, too, from the way he slept on his back, arms flung wide, to his grouchy mood if awakened before he was ready.

But *living together*? No, he was just staying for a time,

then would move on.

"It's not like you're implying," she whispered.

"It could be. Do you want it to be?" His voice was seductive, sexy, suggestive.

Yes! If he would only—

"No!" Shannon scrambled back, out of danger, standing so abruptly her chair fell over and hit the floor with a loud crash. She spun and raced from the room, afraid of where her own thoughts were leading her. She heard his laughter as she slammed her bedroom door. Her heart pounded, hot blood coursed through her and her mind wouldn't relinquish the image of them together. She was so mad she could spit!

Shannon awoke the next morning determined to maintain a serene facade before Jase, no matter how he tempted her. She'd lain awake long into the night, hearing his words echo over and over.

One tiny part of her longed to make them true. She'd love to live with him, share her life with him, build a future together. But the bitter reality was, she could never trust him. She'd never trust a cowboy again.

The coffee had been made by the time she reached the kitchen. A dirty cup sat in the sink. Wandering over to the open door, she looked out into the yard. Jase stood near his truck, talking with Gary. The horse trailer had been unhitched and pushed to one side. Wondering what they were discussing, Shannon stood in the doorway, straining to catch some words, but they were too far away.

While she debated whether to join them or not, Gary laughed and nodded, turning toward the barn. Jase climbed into his truck and started the engine. He drove off without noticing Shannon.

She watched as the dust settled behind him, wondering where he was going so early in the morning. Turning back to the kitchen, she was relieved he had left Shadow and the trailer. At least he'd be back. Until then she hadn't realized how much she'd feared he would up and leave. Which was stupid, he was going to leave in a few weeks. It wouldn't matter if he left early.

Yes, it would.

When she worked at the morning chores with Gary, she casually asked him where Jase had gone.

"Into town. Had some things to see to, he said," Gary replied easily as he helped fork out the fouled straw.

"Did he mention what?" Shannon asked.

"No, just said he'd be back later. You need him to run some errands for you?"

"Uh, no. Just wondered when he'd be back."

"Before supper, I reckon. He tell you about the plans for growing hay?"

"Yes." Shannon discussed the new idea halfheartedly, her curiosity rampant about what errands Jase had.

As the day progressed, Shannon grew more and more distracted as she listened for the sound of Jase's truck returning. Unable to concentrate on anything, she turned to baking to wile away the hours. The gingerbread was ready to come out of the oven when she finally heard his truck. Spaghetti sauce simmered on the stove, garlic bread stood ready to be heated.

Flicking a glance out the window, she turned to pull out the fragrant cake. Cleaning up the last of the bowls and wiping down the counter to give herself something to do, she waited for Jase to come in.

"Something smells good." His easy comment annoyed her. She wanted to know where he had been and why he hadn't told her he was going into town. She'd been worried about him and he walked in as casual as he pleased.

"Gingerbread," she said shortly.

He paused, his hat still in his hand, and looked at her, studying her tense stance, her snapping eyes.

Slowly his lips lifted in that grin that wreaked so much havoc on her equilibrium. "Something wrong, darlin'?" he drawled, tossing the hat on the table and walking over to her.

"No. I didn't know you were going to be gone all day. It's almost supper time." Her voice was tight with suppressed emotion.

"I should have told you I was going into town, but you were still asleep when I left." His hand came up to brush against her cheek.

She knocked it away. "I was not. I saw you drive off."

"Well, you must have just gotten up then. Next time I'll wait until you're awake. I told Gary to tell you." He sounded so reasonable her anger grew.

"He did."

"So what's the problem?"

"Why did you go to town?" She bit her lower lip. Damn, she hadn't wanted to subject him to an inquisition. It wasn't her business and if he told her so it would be no more than she deserved.

Instead, he grinned again. "What's the matter, darlin', you think I went into town to duck work for the day? Cut out to play?"

"No." But she had. She'd thought exactly that. Bobby never could stay on the ranch more than a few days before he had to find some action.

"Yes, you do." His hand encircled her neck beneath her braid and gently rubbed the tight muscles. "I went in to talk to the sheriff about your theft. Then I went to buy a computer. You need to get things automated to cut down on the work, and give you instant access to information. Next I stopped in at the cattleman's association and got the current price of beef. I had my bank wire-transfer the money into your account. I now own three hundred head of that cattle on the range. Now we need to figure out how much land I need to lease till winter."

His fingers slowly massaged her skin. Tingling shivers of awareness pulsated in rhythm with her heart. Heat began to spread from his hand to every cell in her body. She began to soften, weaken, longed to move against the strength before her and lean on him. Yet she knew that way lay danger. He was too potent for her. She was too fragile and afraid to take a chance.

"I'll make you a bill of sale after dinner," she said stiffly, clamping down tightly on the emotions that threatened to spill over.

"It can wait until tomorrow. After dinner we're going back to town."

"Why?"

"To have a little fun. I noticed The Big Bonanza on the square when I drove through town today. They've got a live band tonight so I thought we could go in and dance some."

She stepped back, breaking his hold. "I don't dance." She turned back to the counter, testing the gingerbread, moving to the stove to stir the spaghetti sauce.

"Besides, I don't have time to be going into bars and partying the night away. I have a ranch to run," she added. Was that all rodeo cowboys thought about, having a good time?

"You don't seem to have time for fun at all," he said, leaning against the counter, crossing his arms across his chest, the cast already turning dull from the dirt on the ranch.

"I have a ranch to run, responsibilities—"

"Dammit, Shannon, you make it sound like a sacred quest. Everyone around these parts has a ranch to run, but that doesn't mean they can't break loose once in a while and have fun. I haven't seen you relax since I got here."

"You do enough for both of us," she said petulantly. "Bobby always did."

"Yeah, well maybe you drove him to it," Jase snapped.

She looked up, stunned.

His eyes were dark, angry. His gaze didn't waver as she faced him, despite the hurt and uncertainty in hers.

"I didn't," she whispered.

"How do I know that? If you were as righteous then as now, as concerned about the ranch over the relationship with your husband, maybe you did."

She blinked back the sudden tears, unable to believe what she was hearing.

"Listen to me, Shannon. I don't mean to hurt you, I only want to make a point. There's more to life, more to building a marriage, than just work. The ranch is important, I'm not saying it isn't. But a well-rounded life includes friends and fun and laughter. You work too hard. You need a break, something frivolous and fun. You'll end up burning out, otherwise. I know. I was there for years."

"And you're trying to make up for it all now, I suppose."

"In a way, yeah, that's exactly what I'm doing. I had more responsibility than I wanted or deserved for my age. I was seventeen when my folks died. Seventeen! Shannon, I should have been thinking about girls and dances and school. Instead I worried about bills and money to buy clothes for my brother and sister and where our next meal would come from. By the time they were settled, I had nothing left to give the ranch. I needed time just for me. I know you think it's selfish and self-centered, but I need it. One day I won't. One day I'll get life back in balance and take up ranching again. But until then I plan to have all the fun I can cram into the day."

"And I suppose I should join you in that fun," she said bitterly, wanting to turn away, caught by his hard stare.

"In some of it," he said slowly. "For the time I'm here. What can one night out a week hurt? We'll go in to town and see your neighbors. Dance to the band. Have a few laughs."

She shook her head.

He sighed. "All right. I'm leaving at seven. If you want to come with me, I'd like that. If not, I'm still going." He pushed away and headed for his bedroom. In only a few minutes, Shannon heard the shower.

"Getting all cleaned up for a night on the town," she muttered, and she stirred the sauce recklessly. Cutting up the gingerbread, she put two large servings on a plate and carried it over to Gary and Dink.

A night on the town. The words echoed over and over. How long had it been since she'd gone out?

Before Bobby had died. Long before.

She didn't linger with the hired hands, only smiling at their appreciation for the cake before going to the corral to watch the horses. It wasn't her night to feed them, but she watched as they ambled over to the fence.

Was there a grain of truth in what Jase had said? Had she driven Bobby to the lengths he'd gone before he died? She had tried to be a good wife. She had tried to make a home for them while he was out riding the broncs and the bulls.

They'd started off fine. At first she had traveled the circuit with him. Life had been carefree and full of mindless excursions into the fun side of things. But she'd grown tired of constant games. She'd longed for stability, something solid to build a future on. Bobby hadn't wanted to leave the rodeo. Thinking back, she remembered nagging him to stay home, harping on working the ranch, building it up. Had that been only her dream? Had Bobby wanted something else? Had she driven him away by her holy quest to create the home she had always wanted?

No, Bobby hadn't been driven away. But he had had little to come home for, except a load of complaints and suggestions that would take him away from what he truly loved.

Guiltily, Shannon acknowledged she hadn't gone with him when he asked, thinking the ranch more important. Even the months Bobby worked on the ranch, and went into town on Saturday nights, she'd been too tired, too concerned about what needed doing the next day to bother to go into town with him. She hadn't wanted to be considered as frivolous as she considered her husband.

And she had done them both a disservice. Bobby couldn't help what he was any more than she could help being who she was. He'd bought the ranch at her request and had truly tried to satisfy her. But he had had his own agenda for life and it probably had not included a wife and ranch to tie him down.

Was she only realizing it now?

She knew they should not have married. The love they shared had burned hot and bright and quickly faded. The last year they had tried to make things work, but only as strangers, not as lovers.

Maybe she wasn't cut out for marriage. Maybe she was destined to be a single woman rancher. Would this place become her whole life? Was she not destined to have children, to share the good times and bad with someone special?

Slowly she walked to the house. Jase's words had hurt, but they had also purged. It was time for her to start building her life anew, and do it right, this time.

Five

J ase stared at himself in the mirror, swiped clear from the steam. Open mouth, insert both feet, he thought. He'd been hard on Shannon and she hadn't deserved it. He didn't know anything about her life with Bobby Blackstone. And it was none of his business anyway. She was trying hard to make a go of things. He should cut her some slack.

Lathering his cheeks, he frowned.

He could remember the days—and nights—when he worried endlessly about taking care of his siblings, of keeping the ranch from falling apart and about losing the only home he'd ever known.

Did Shannon have the same fears? He knew she did.

But he also knew, from his own experience, that she needed to round out her life. To his knowledge, no friends had called her. She didn't have a computer so wasn't hanging out with friends on Facebook, or exchanging emails.

And they had not left the ranch once in the week he'd been here until his trip to town.

Trying to justify his words wasn't working. He'd seen the hurt he'd inflicted and it made him sick. She was trying so hard. He felt as if he'd kicked her when she was down.

Bobby was a wild cowboy. A no-holds-barred kind of reckless rider that attracted buckle bunnies like no one else. And Jase had never seen him turn one away.

Like anything, if there were faults, it was probably on both sides.

He swiped the razor against his cheeks. He'd wanted her to go to town. He was doing better and a night out with others sounded like fun. He didn't know how much he could dance, but one or two slow songs with her in his arms couldn't hurt.

He rinsed the razor. Who was he kidding, it would be like torture, holding her, smelling that sweet scent she wore, touching that sexy body would drive him bonkers.

He grinned at his reflection. But what a way to go.

Only, his grin faded, she'd said no. If there was any dancing tonight it would be with strangers. And that held no appeal at all.

He was all dressed up, was her first thought when Jase joined her at the table for dinner. *He'd even shaved again.* Surreptitiously she took in the fresh shirt, clean jeans and the scent of his after-shave lotion. His hair was still damp, neatly combed. She longed to run her fingers through it and mess it up. She liked it when his hair fell any which way because of wearing his hat or from the way his fingers dragged through it.

Ignoring the awkwardness she felt, she gathered her courage.

"Jase," she said.

If he made a snide comment at her change of mind, she didn't know what she'd do.

"Yeah?" He looked up from the stew, his eyes silvery in the light, catching hers as he waited to hear what she was going to say.

"If it's all right, I'd like to go in to town with you tonight. I'll change as soon as the dishes are done." She held her breath. Had he changed his mind?

Slowly he smiled and nodded. "I'll wait."

"But this is not a date," she added quickly.

He raised one eyebrow. "Did I ever say it was? It's merely two business associates going into town to visit neighbors."

She flushed slightly, hearing the amusement in his tone. She dropped her gaze to her meal, feeling the flush of embarrassment rise. She should have kept her mouth shut. He'd never thought of it as a date, she should not have, either.

"I saw the sheriff today when I went into town," Jase said a moment later.

"So you said. Why?" Grateful for the change of topic, Shannon quickly picked it up.

"I wanted to learn a bit more about Rod Thompson and just what the sheriff had done to apprehend him."

"Not much he can do from what he told me. Rod skipped. No trace."

"Yeah, he said that. Also that Rod had a problem gambling."

"Gambling?"

"You didn't know?"

She shook her head.

"Seems like he had a seriously big loss. Probably saw the money from the ranch as an out."

"So he stole it from me to pay a gambling debt?" She couldn't believe it. All her hard work over the last several years gone, just to satisfy a man's gambling debts?

"Word on the street is that he didn't pay the debt, the sheriff said. He probably planned to, but once he had the money in hand he changed his mind and just took off with it instead. The sheriff said he's notified all the surrounding states and is searching for him here in Texas but he doesn't hold out much hope. If the man's a compulsive gambler, he's probably blown the wad already, and still owes the fellows here."

"So while I slave away trying to make a go of it, he's off spending my money *gambling*! I wish I didn't know. Or had known before. I knew he went into town several nights a week. But his work around here was so good, I didn't question it."

"He could have been courting a girl. You couldn't have known."

"I should have." Frustration colored her voice. "Doesn't any man have a sense of responsibility? Do they all just want to play their entire lives?" She shoved back her chair and carried her dish to the sink, plopping it down hard and running hot water over it.

Jase came up behind her, his right hand reaching for her shoulder. "Hey, lighten up. Did your father play all the time?"

"Sure. He was a pilot. They're notorious for hard living and hard playing. When he wasn't up in the air, he spent his time at the O-club, boasting of exploits with the other jet jockeys. Everywhere we went I tried to make a home for us and he left me to it. Every base was the same. He never mistreated me, but he ignored me, seeking fun and games over spending time at home."

"Honey, you've had a raw deal with men. They aren't all like that," he said gently, rubbing her shoulder.

"All the ones I meet are," she said. "Isn't there someone out there that would put home and hearth before fun and pleasure?"

"Most people do. Most people find home and hearth provide the pleasure."

"Maybe, but not the men I meet."

"Then tonight we'll see if you can meet some other kind of man."

She shut off the water and turned. Jase's arm encircled her, drew her up against his long, lean body. Resting her hands against his chest, she looked up into his eyes. For an instant she felt sheltered and safe. His strength was evident, even as she knew his steadfastness was questionable. She longed to lose herself with him. To explore the future with a strong man beside her.

But he wasn't that man.

His heart thudded beneath her hand while the heat from his body slowly enveloped her. His breath stirred tendrils of her hair as his scent filled her nostrils, spicy and male, intoxicating. Slowly she relaxed, leaned against him, tilting her head back for the kiss that was inevitable. The one she wanted as much as he did.

His lips were warm, firm, hungry, moving across her mouth in a sweeping caress, touching her, possessing her.

His tongue traced her lips, rubbing again and again against the seam until she opened her mouth to permit him access. He tugged against her lower lip, skimmed the soft skin of her lower lip, grazed against her teeth.

Her heartbeat rampant in her chest, blood rushed through her veins, scalding every inch of her. She snuggled against him, longing for more, longing for him to deepen the kiss. Her hands tightened into fists, clutching his shirt as if dragging him closer still. His arm tightened, her own were caught between them. She struggled to get even closer.

On and on the sweet kiss continued, each straining to give the utmost pleasure to the other within the confines of a single, hot kiss.

When she moaned softly in her delight, Jase slowed down. He drew back enough to see her dazed expression, her dreamy eyes, softly swollen lips, glaze of color high in her cheeks.

Groaning he buried his face against her neck, drinking in the sweet scent of her. "God, honey, I want you!"

Sanity returned slowly. For endless moments Shannon remained in his embrace, savoring the feel of his body against hers, savoring the heat that pounded through her. For one long moment she savored the dream of the two of them together, playing.

Then reality returned.

"To play with," she whispered sadly. She pushed away, her fingers lingering for a moment as she tried to brush out the wrinkles she'd caused in his fresh shirt. Reluctant to end the fairy-tale embrace that meant

different things to her than to him, she stayed a moment
longer in his warm embrace.

He released her. His eyes were hooded, his
expression impossible to read. "There's a time for play,
Shannon."

"Yes, there is. I'm going to change now. I'll be ready
in a few minutes. Have some gingerbread. I kept it
warm."

She pushed past him and hurried to her room. Her
senses were inflamed, heightened. Colors seemed more
vibrant. The air was scented with grass and dust and
cattle overlaid with the hint of Jase's aftershave. The soft
air caressed her as she hurried into the shower. The
water was silky as it cascaded across her heated skin.

She had to draw in her raging emotions, stomp
down her craving for the man. She knew he was not for
her and she'd be a fool to believe it was any different.
Even for a minute.

She couldn't deny the sexual attraction between
them. But that's all it was. She wouldn't fall for another
cowboy.

She couldn't survive another heartbreak.

It was the shortest shower on record. Once she
finished, she put on fresh underwear and went to her
closet. Pushing one dress aside, she studied another.
Then another. Suddenly she realized what she was doing.

"This is not a date!" she repeated aloud. Turning,
she pulled a clean pair of jeans from her drawer. They
were new, still stiff. She took a baby blue cotton shirt
from the hanger and drew it on. It buttoned up the front
and she was satisfied Jase would not suspect she dressed

up at all for him.

Brushing her hair, she left it to fall down her back. Because of being in the braid all day, it was wavy and shiny as she brushed through the thickness. Two clips on either side kept it from falling into her face.

As she put on a light touch of makeup, she tried to quell the flutters in her stomach. It was not a date, she repeated as she studied herself in the full-length mirror.

She was pleased to note that she looked fine. The blouse enhanced the smoky blue of her eyes, brought a touch of color to her cheeks. Or had Jase's kiss done that? Her clothes were clean, neat, and nicer than she wore around the ranch, yet they were not at all dressy. No one could get the wrong idea from what she wore.

Certainly not Jase, if his expression was anything to go by when she joined him a few minutes later in the kitchen. He glanced up, then back to his coffee.

"I'm ready."

"I see. Just let me finish this cup. The gingerbread was good."

"Thanks." She glanced around, surprised. All the dishes had been washed and put away.

"Jase, thank you. You didn't have to clean up."

He shrugged. "No problem."

She turned back to him, amazed. She couldn't ever remember her father or husband doing dishes. They had considered it woman's work. She watched as he finished his cup of coffee, his throat working as he swallowed. She longed to touch that brown column, feel the pulse of his heart beneath hers. Taking a deep breath, she headed for the door before she made a fool of herself.

It's not a date, she repeated over and over as Jase drove into Tumbleweed. They talked little, both content with their own thoughts, though Shannon wondered if his were as chaotic as hers. Turning to look out the window, she tasted her lips with her tongue, wondering if she were imagining his taste lingered. Closing her eyes brought back the sweet sensations he'd wrought. Opening them dispensed them only marginally.

Jase turned into the street that ran along one side of the downtown square in Tumbleweed. The place was full. Cars and pickup trucks crammed into every available space. Parking was impossible. He turned up a side street near The Big Bonanza and found a spot.

Shannon thrust open her own door before he could offer to let her out. *This was not a date.*

But she had trouble remembering that in the next instant. When he joined her on the sidewalk, his good arm came around her shoulders, his hand cupping her shoulder, one finger beneath the collar against her bare skin. He pulled her gently to him, so her left shoulder snuggled against his hard chest. His right hand steered her slightly ahead of him as they walked to the bar.

The sounds filled the night; laughter, noisy talk, the clink of glasses. The closer they came to the bar, the louder the noises. When Jase reached around her and pushed open the door, the din spilled over them like a tangible wave. The air was slightly smoky, the atmosphere one of good humor and fun.

At first Shannon thought the entire town was present, but as they moved through the crowd, searching for an empty table or booth, she realized she recognized most of the men and women present. Smiling and nodding or waving to those who called her, she began to relax.

Jase found one of only a couple of tables still vacant. He drew his chair right up to hers, and rested his arm across the back of hers in a proprietorial manner.

"Really, Jase," she said, turning amused eyes on him. "You act as if you're staking your claim."

"Exactly that, darlin'," he drawled, smiling down into her eyes.

"This isn't a date," she said quickly, her heart fluttering at his look.

His hand came under her chin, tilting her head back until her face was close to his. "Where I come from, if a man brings a woman to a dance, she stays with him. I expect the same here. If you want to pretend this is not a date, but a business meeting, we'll talk about cattle." There was a hint of steel in his tone.

"What'll you have, folks?" The young waitress dressed in fancy fringed Western wear smiled down at them. She held a tray at her waist and leaned over to put napkins on their table.

"Beer," Jase said, raising his eyebrow at Shannon.

At her nod, he amended, "Two beers."

"Right away."

Shannon watched the waitress wind her way through the crowd.

"Relax, Shannon, I'm not going to eat you, much as I want to sometimes," Jase muttered.

Just then a cheer went up through the crowd as the band came in and started setting up their equipment. Jase reached out and captured Shannon's hand and laced his fingers through hers, resting them on his hard thigh.

She glanced at him briefly, but said nothing, turning back to study the others in the large country-western bar.

She only pretended to ignore him, to ignore the sizzling tremors that raced up her arm, that tantalized her, teased her. She was more conscious of his hand than she had been of anything else in her life. Trying to breathe became a chore. Trying to give the impression of disinterest and serenity became a monumental task.

Brad Chalmers and his wife Charlene spotted them and came over to speak to Shannon. She introduced Jase and soon they dragged over two chairs and sat. The four of them chatted casually. If the Chalmers noticed anything amiss with Jase holding her hand, they made no comment, though Shannon noted they glanced at their linked hands rather pointedly at one point.

When the beer arrived, Jase released her long enough to take a long pull directly from the bottle. Then he recaptured her hand, his cold from the beer. Shannon tried to relax, enjoying the feel of his hand around hers, his fingers thrust between hers, the soft rubbing of his thumb across the back of her hand.

In fact, she began to enjoy the entire evening. It was good to have a bit of fun. She'd been working too long on the ranch, bound up in worries about the future.

The Chalmers beckoned to another couple to join them and soon their table expanded. Laughter and quick rejoinders flowed among them all and time flew by.

When the band started their first set, Jase tugged at her hand, pulling her up from the chair.

"Really, Jase, I don't dance very well," she said, hesitating, pulling back.

He ignored her and led her onto the wooden dance floor. "Honey, no one here is judging the dancing. We'll have a good time, that's all." The number was lively and before she could protest, he swung her into his arms and into the rhythm of the music. Despite the cast, despite the taped ribs, he danced with enthusiasm and skill.

Just like he did everything, she thought briefly, surprised to find out how much she liked it. After only two stumbles, she caught the rhythm and had no trouble keeping up with Jase.

When the song ended, another cowboy asked Shannon to dance. Involuntarily she sought Jase's permission. He nodded easily, grinned at her and turned to find another partner.

Time flew by as they danced song after song. Shannon talked with the cowboys and ranchers who danced with her, caught up on local news, and explained who Jase was and how he was helping her. Most had heard of Rod's theft and commiserated with her.

When the band began a slow song, Jase appeared and drew her away from Josh McKensie, a younger son of one of the big ranchers south of Tumbleweed.

"Slow dances are mine," Jase explained to the younger man as he drew Shannon up against him. His cast made it awkward, so he simply wrapped his arms around her and held her in his embrace. Slowly they moved to the soft strains of the love song.

"That was rude," Shannon said softly, moving in step with him, feeling his thighs brush with hers, relishing the sensation of his arms banded around her, holding her as if she were precious.

"Rude be damned. For future reference, slow dances are mine."

"Jase—"

"Don't argue, Shannon." He rested his cheek against her hair and swayed with the music.

Giving herself up to the pleasure of being in his arms, she fell quiet. She was warm from exercise, he was equally warm, yet the heat that grew between them had little to do with the fast pace of the previous dances.

His legs brushed by hers, one came between hers, moved away, as tantalizing as deliberate seduction. Shannon was mesmerized by the sensations that swept through her. The sizzling attraction that flared between them was heightened by the sensual seduction of the slow, sweet love song. His body moved against hers, moved her with him, choreographed to offer the most in delightful intimacy.

"Careful, darlin'," he said in a low, husky voice.

The realization of her power welled up deep within her. This virile sexy man wanted her. Her, Shannon Blackstone. The woman who had not been able to keep her husband home for months on end. She glowed with the sensation, happiness bubbling up and threatening to engulf her forever.

Standing on tiptoes, she dragged her body against his, reveling in the response he was unable to deny. Sweetly, she kissed his cheek.

"Honey, if you don't stop, I'm going to ignore your refusals and find a quiet place for us to end this."

She tried to pull away, giving them some space, but his arms refused to release her. He smiled and dropped a light kiss on her lips just as the song ended and the singer announced the band would take a brief break.

Reluctantly Jase set her away from him, close enough to shelter him from other eyes, but breaking contact with her. "You like to flirt with danger, is that it, Ms. Blackstone?"

"Am I in danger, Mr. Hart?" she sassed up at him, her hands still on his shoulders as if she couldn't let go, couldn't release the bond that held them.

"Keep it up and see," he threatened.

She laughed and glanced away as heat suffused her cheeks.

He chuckled and tilted up her chin until her eyes met his again.

"Now why should you be embarrassed? I'm the one with the problem."

Someone jostled them as they cleared the floor, and he turned her around, holding her before him, and guided her toward their table.

"Sometimes you scare me, darlin'. You're all grown up, married, widowed, and yet sometimes you act as innocent as a new babe. Let's visit with these fine folks who've joined us and forget what you and I both want so bad I can taste it."

Shannon sank down gratefully in her chair, glad for the rest. Jase drove her crazy. She longed to be with him, spend time with him, talking, dancing, kissing.

Yet she was not so foolish the second time around. She knew where sweet-talking cowboys got you. She knew better than to trust her heart and future to a man bent on enjoying life to the fullest. Home and stability were too hard earned, too important to blow away with a will-o'-the-wisp emotion like infatuation for a slick rodeo cowboy who wanted a good time.

Telling herself that was easier than believing it. As the evening wore on, the pattern was set. She danced almost every dance. But the slow ones were Jase's alone. Knowing she was playing with fire didn't matter. Each time he took her into his arms, she went willingly. Their bodies met like long-time lovers, moving together in a sensual ballet of touch, brush, stroke. The haunting music heightened her senses and the deep emotion that threatened to overwhelm her every time was as close to love as she'd ever seen.

But still she denied it.

It was late when the band played its last number. Later still by the time Shannon and Jase said goodbye to the couples they'd shared the evening with. Feeling tired and happy, Shannon relished Jase's arm around her as they strolled to the truck.

The evening air was crisp, cool. The sky a dark, velvet quilt that shimmered with a million stars in the heavens. The town was still and quiet, only the sound of the cars starting up and leaving disturbed the stillness.

Jase helped Shannon into the truck, leaned in after her, his arm heavy against her waist.

"I had a good time, Jase. I'm glad you asked me," she said.

"I'm glad you came."

He leaned forward and kissed her. It was gentle.

Slowly, Shannon's fingers traced down his face, feeling the smooth, warm skin.

"If you hadn't brought me, you might have scored with one of the other women," she said against his lips, smiling at the thought. Had he shaved and dressed up to find a girl?

"I scored big time dancing with you, darlin'," he said, his tongue rubbing over her lips lightly. He kissed her again and straightened, slamming the door and moving around to his side.

Shannon's elation soared. He'd been glad to be with her.

Smiling dreamily, she closed her eyes, remembering every dance, every conversation. It had been a long time since she'd had such fun. Maybe Jase was right, she was too one-sided. Henceforth she'd try to make time every week to do something totally frivolous. With that thought uppermost, she drifted to sleep before they left Tumbleweed.

When Shannon awoke the next morning she was in bed, still wearing her shirt! She sat up, and stared around her, remembering nothing beyond leaving the dance. How had she gotten into bed? Her jeans and boots were off, though she had no memory of discarding them. Closing her eyes, she lay back against her pillow with a plop.

The warm delicious feelings of the previous night now gave way to regrets and embarrassment. How could she have behaved so wantonly with Jase? What kind of signals had she sent out, plastering herself against him when they danced, receiving his kisses? Returning those kisses.

So much for her fine talk about not starting anything between them. She'd practically begged him to make love to her.

It had to be the beer, though she'd only had two all night long. Or maybe it was a full moon and she'd been bewitched. Slowly she opened her eyes and took a deep breath. Now all she had to do was face Jase, and make sure he knew there was nothing between them. Could be nothing between them, no matter how she acted when they went dancing.

Full of good intentions, she was annoyed when she stormed out of her room later fully dressed and ready to do battle, to find Jase had gone out with Dink to work on some fencing. True to his word, he'd left her a message on the kitchen table. They weren't expected back before late afternoon.

Grateful for the delay, Shannon admitted she'd be better able to cope with some time without Jase around.

She went to the office to set up the computer. Maybe she'd try to figure out the accounting program he'd bought and get started on inputting data.

At least she started out with that goal. But as the day dragged on, she wasn't so sure. Setting up the computer had been a snap. Even loading the program. Then she began to read the on-line instructions and felt overwhelmed. What should she do first? Set up accounts for routing expenses like feed and farrier? Begin tracking the number of heads of cattle? She wasn't sure she'd do it right. He must know this program, would she be wasting time only to have him come in and show her a different way?

Try as she might to make sense of the bloodlines of the cattle she was raising, to test her newly acquired knowledge on plans for rotating stock on the range, her thoughts drifted back to Jase time after time. She could recall every detail since she watched him fly off that horse at the rodeo. She remembered every word he'd said to her, every brush of his fingers against her, every aspect of each kiss they'd shared.

She realized she liked him. Liked being around him, liked being the object of his gentle teasing. Liked his touching her.

By mid afternoon she was fast drawing to the conclusion she was falling in love with him despite her best intentions to avoid such an entanglement at all costs. She refused give in to the feelings blossoming through her. She'd enjoy his company while he was here, then wish him well.

Who was she kidding? If this continued, she'd miss him to death when he left!

She sat back in the desk chair, all thoughts of ranch business gone.

Stunned, she realized she was in real danger of a broken heart. She was starting to want to share a life with him. She didn't want to go on alone forever. Jase was the most exciting, kind, generous man she knew. Not to mention the most sexy.

And the most irresponsible.

He made no pretense to be any different. He'd never

even hinted he wanted anything to do with her beyond the few weeks he'd agreed to help. How could she be so dumb to even consider a man who charmed his way through life and rode on to the next event with a casual disregard for responsibilities and other people as he did?

A brief infatuation, that's all it was.

She would not fall in love with Jase Hart!

Six

As if to prove to herself the truth of what she was saying, Shannon decided to ride out and see how Jase and Dink were faring on the fence, maybe even give them a hand. She was done with paperwork for the day. Time she delved into the more practical aspects about her ranch.

Packing a jug of cold lemonade and several tin cups, Shannon cut up the rest of the gingerbread and went to saddle her horse.

The sun blazed hot overhead, the air windy and dry. The sky was crystal clear, yet there was an odd unsettled feeling in the air. Would they have a storm? With the low humidity and the gusts of winds, she felt uneasy. Adjusting her hat to shade her eyes from the glare, she headed toward the section of the ranch Jase said they'd be working. She moved easily with the horse, knowing she rode well for someone who had only learned a few years earlier. While she'd never acquire the proficiency Jase displayed when working with Shadow, she knew she was more than adequate for the work her ranch entailed.

She loved outdoor work. Riding gave her pleasure, as well as pride in her accomplishments. She'd participated in the last couple of roundups, moved portions of her herd from one grazing pasture to another, spent endless hours riding the perimeter checking on fencing. She enjoyed being outside, good weather or bad.

In the distance she saw the dusty pickup truck and beyond that the two men working on the fencing. Riding slowly, anticipation began to build. *She'd see him in another few moments.* Recognizing that the shimmering feelings that rose when around him were only signs of an infatuation that would quickly fade once he'd left, she tried to ignore them.

Maybe she should change her tactics and let herself enjoy the oddity of the sensations he inspired for the short time he would work at her ranch. Maybe she should take what he offered, knowing it was only temporary with nothing serious at the end.

Could she do that?

She urged her mount into a faster gait, anxious to see Jase again.

Dink hammered in the clip while Jase pulled the strands of wire taut. In the hot afternoon air Jase had discarded his shirt. His muscles bulged as he stretched the wire. The ace bandages around his ribs stood out in stark contrast to the deep copper of his tanned chest. His cast was getting dirtier by the day.

Shannon drew up near the truck and dismounted, ground hitching her horse.

"Hi, I brought you guys a snack." She yanked off her saddlebags and walked over to them.

For a moment depression threatened. Two-thirds of her ranch hands were here, one old enough to be her grandfather, the other injured. It was a sad state of affairs when her ranch was reduced to such a crew.

Shaking off the feeling, she pinned a smile on her face. At least they were working, for which she was grateful. And this was only a temporary situation. Once she had some working capital she'd be able to hire cowboys as needed.

Once things turned around, she'd start building up her herd again.

She forgot about her plans for the future as she became achingly aware of Jase. Fascinated by the raw essence of masculinity before her, she couldn't resist skimming her glance across his broad shoulders, chancing a peek at his chest. Perspiration gleamed in the hot sun, the sheen coating his tanned skin like a warm, glistening polish. A drop formed near one male nipple, slithered slowly down. Captivated, Shannon stared, mesmerized, tracking it on its slow journey until it was absorbed by the ace bandages. She swallowed.

"You're a lifesaver," Jase said easily, waiting for Dink to finish hammering the last fastener before turning to walk over to Shannon. He reseated his hat on his head, tipping it forward slightly as he stared at her.

"You all right?" He reached out to brush his knuckles down her flushed cheek.

Blinking to break the spell, Shannon nodded, turning to greet Dink with enthusiasm she hoped masked the thundering in her head.

How could she gawk at the man like she'd never seen one before? Just because he personified the perfect male physique was no reason to act like a star-struck teenager.

"The lemonade is cold and the gingerbread is still fresh," she said, darting another quick glance at Jase.

"Your timing's perfect. We need a break," Jase said easily. "Right, Dink?"

"I don't mind sitting a spell." The older man took his cup and a piece of cake and went to sit in the scant shade of the pickup. Jase stood by Shannon, sipping from the tin cup, steadily watching her over the rim.

"This is nice," he said.

She nodded, nervously looking around. "Should you be doing this? I mean, with your ribs and all."

Darn, she felt as nervous as a rabbit faced with a coyote. She took a deep breath, let it out slowly.

"It needs doing."

"But with your injuries—"

"I'm fine. Dink's doing most of the work."

She glanced over and saw the older man had closed his eyes. Was he already taking a cat nap? She knew Jase gave more credit to the older man than warranted. He was nice that way.

She brought herself up sharp. She was not looking for things to admire about Jase Hart. She was trying to talk herself out of her infatuation, not feed it.

"Won't you get sunburned?" she asked, unable to resist sliding her glance over his muscular chest again. Her fingers longed to trace his muscles, tangle gently with the faint dusting of golden curly hair. It took real effort to face forward and watch the sun glitter off the water as the river near the boundary rushed on its journey.

"Too hot for a shirt. I've half a mind to just plunge into the river and cool off all over," Jase said as they reached the bank.

"Not here. This is where cattle drink. There's a nice spot a mile or so upriver. Sometimes I go swimming there," she said.

She wished she had taken a cup of lemonade. It would give her something to do with her hands.

"Want to go swimming now?" he asked whimsically.

"I don't have a suit," she said without thinking.

"So? I don't, either." From the amusement evident in his tone, she knew he was teasing her.

"Not today, thanks," she replied primly, closing her eyes against the images that danced before her.

He laughed. "Yeah, I figured you'd say something like that, darlin'. All work, right?"

Her eyes snapped open, the vision gone. Reality returned. "No, but not all play, either."

"You've got that right. You ever planning on getting married again?" he asked.

Surprised at the question, she turned to face him. "Not necessarily. I don't have much opportunity to meet too many men."

"You danced with a parcel of them last night."

"They were fine to dance with, but…I don't know."

"Yeah, you need to be looking for a responsible man that works all the time."

"That's not fair, Jase. I don't want someone who works all the time. But I need someone who puts duty before feckless pleasure. I need to know he'd be someone I could count on to be home when needed and not out chasing after other women all in the name of a good time."

"Damn, he hurt you bad." He looked away, pensive.

Shannon held perfectly still. Bobby had hurt her.

Rod had hurt her in a different way.

Would Jase hurt her, as well?

She had to guard her heart. Yet she was more attracted to him than she had been to her husband. How did she explain that? How long would Jase go on seeking fun and adventure to the exclusion of all else? Would the habit become so ingrained he'd never change?

Would anyone give him the chance at a steady job when he was through with the rodeos? Or would he drift from one place to another, always looking for an easy way out, more concerned for idle pleasure than the satisfaction of a job well done?

"Do you ever plan to marry?" she asked, curious about his future, a little sad she'd not figure in that future.

He shrugged. "Maybe. But that would be a long time down the road. I have other things I want to do first. Hell, I already feel I've done my share raising kids. I had my brother and sister for years."

"Now you need to make up for the fun you missed as a kid," she murmured, suddenly empathizing with him. He'd been only a teenager himself when his parents died. He'd missed out on a lot.

"Yeah. There is that. Come on, I want to get this section finished today. Dink's had enough of a rest."

Without waiting to see if she would follow, Jase turned and headed back to the portion of the fence they were replacing. Dink joined him at his call and the two set to work.

Shannon watched for a while, then joined in, taking turns banging the clips against the posts to hold the barbed wire Jase pulled so taut. Dink untangled the old wire, baled it for removal. No sense leaving it where cattle could get tangled.

Jase was hard to get a handle on, she thought as she worked. He disclaimed all responsibility, but she started to wonder if that were true. He pulled his weight around the ranch. More than his share, if truth be told. Especially as he was still healing from his injuries.

He was lavish in complimenting the older men and their contributions. He took his role as teacher seriously, telling her what she needed to know, pointing out articles and books that would assist that process.

Last night had been the first occasion since he'd been here that he'd gone into town for fun. While it had been just over a week since he arrived, he'd done more in the time he'd been on the ranch than Bobby had done when he visited.

Visited. That was the crux of the entire situation. Jase was only visiting. Soon he'd move on and she'd be left behind.

Taking a deep breath, Shannon turned away from the sudden longing she had to learn more about him, find out more about him to like. She needed distance, as much as she could put between them. To ease the pain when he left.

When they were finished, she caught up her horse and mounted.

"See you at dinner," she called.

Jase acknowledged her with a wave as she rode back to the ranch house, climbing in beside Dink and settling back for the return ride.

He was beat. He didn't want to admit it, or let Shannon know. But he'd give anything to get a stiff drink and hit the hay.

"You doing okay?" Dink asked, as the truck bounced over the rough terrain.

Jase gritted his teeth against the pain. "I will be when we get back and I get out of this blasted truck. I think you missed a bump back there a bit."

Dink chuckled and slowed down. "Sorry, I wanted to get back soon. Gary's bringing pizza tonight. I like it semi-hot, not stone cold."

Jase liked pizza but couldn't get up any interest. He focused on not giving into the pain, and counting the minutes until they reached the house.

If Shannon had any idea how much he could be setting back his healing, she'd have his head. He almost smiled remembering she said she was in charge of the men of the ranch. He'd appreciate that more if his ribs didn't hurt like hell.

Dink slowed even more. "You're looking pale," he said.

"Watch where you're driving and don't worry about me."

"You don't have anything to prove to any of us, man. We know you know what you're doing. You've already made a good difference here. Shannon works too hard. She needs a man to handle the rough stuff."

"She has you and Gary for that," Jase said taking a deep breath. He had to make it back to the ranch without passing out in pain. He'd never hear the last of it from Shannon if he didn't.

"Sure, as much as we can do. But both of us would be retired if we had any money. The young guys took off once Rod robbed the place."

Jase frowned. What was Dink getting to?

"And?"

"And nothing, just saying you don't have to half kill yourself to prove anything. I believe you've done more in the week you've been here than Bobby did in six months."

"It was his place."

"And he took it on thinking it would run itself. Believing the money would always come in, he'd win all-around, and be cock of the walk. Then he was killed. No insurance, nothing to take care of his widow."

Jase already knew most of that. Not the part where the man thought the ranch would run itself.

Most cowboys who rode the circuit longed for fame and fortune. And in the twenties they could hardly imagine getting old and not being able to ride.

He probably fell into that category. He was a bit old to be hitting the circuit. Older than most of the competition. But they didn't have the drive and determination he had. He would keep riding until the time was right to stop. A couple of busted ribs and a broken arm wouldn't stop him. Slow him up a bit, but not stop him.

Jase was cleaning up when the phone rang. Shannon turned down the burner and reached for the phone.

"Hello, is Jase Hart there?" a soft, feminine voice asked.

"Yes, hold on, I'll get him." Shannon put the receiver down, wondering who was calling her temporary foreman. Some woman he'd danced with last night, she bet.

"Jase!" she called down the hall. "Phone."

He came out of his room, buttoning his shirt. He was barefoot.

"You can take it in the office if you like," she said, heading back to the kitchen. She lifted the receiver to hear if he'd picked up.

"Hello? Hi, Brie."

She quietly replaced the receiver and turned back to her pan. *Brie?* He was a fast worker. She knew that. He'd only been here a day before he'd first kissed her. And if she'd let him, he'd have gone a lot farther than a kiss.

He was no better than Bobby. Was she to be subjected to numerous phone calls from the women in town who caught his interest?

She'd caught his interest, a tiny voice inside reminded her. He was more than interested. It was she who held back. She shouldn't complain if other women didn't feel that same need to refrain from taking all he offered.

Beating the potatoes vented some of her frustration, some of her jealousy. She had no reason for either emotion. She'd known going into the arrangement what he was. He'd done nothing to change her mind. Good timing cowboy, don't ever forget, she admonished herself.

"Dinner ready?" Jase came into the kitchen and sat down at the table. He'd finished dressing, including his boots. Shannon glared at him.

"Finished with your girlfriend?" she asked sweetly, wanting to slam down the plate of food. Or dump it on his head.

She wished she could eat in her room or with the men.

He raised an eyebrow, rocking back in his chair and studying her. "Miffed about something, darlin'?" he asked.

"No." She sat down and attacked her dinner.

"Curious about my phone call, maybe?" His eyes danced in amusement.

"Not at all. You can have as many calls as you want, as long as it doesn't interfere with your helping me with the ranch. Are you going out tonight?"

She could have bitten her tongue. She didn't want him to think she cared. He could do what he wanted in his off time. She didn't care if he went into town every night of the week.

He chuckled, rocked the chair back down on all four legs and picked up his fork. "Not unless you go with me." He began to eat.

The atmosphere grew tense, Shannon knew it and knew it was her fault. But she was so ...so angry, hurt, confused.

"Why would I want to go with you when I bet *Brie*

would love to go out with you."

"Shannon?"

"What?" She met his gaze.

"That was my sister on the phone. Brianna Hart. We call her Brie."

She opened her mouth to tell him she didn't care. But nothing came out. Snapping it shut, she knew she'd blown it. Closing her eyes, she broke contact with his silvery gaze. She felt like an idiot.

"Oh."

"Yeah, oh. She got my letter telling her where I was and what happened at the rodeo. She was concerned about me."

"Where does she live?" Shannon wanted to sink through the floor or run to her room and hide, never have to face the man again. She felt like an absolute, total and complete idiot! But she held her ground. And there was still the rampant curiosity she felt every time she was around him. Which was most of the time lately.

"She lives in Laramie. Graduated a couple of years ago from the university and got a job in the mathematics department." The pride in her accomplishments sounded in his voice.

"And your brother, where's he?" Shannon asked.

"He works on a ranch in the eastern part of the state." Jase's response seemed a bit guarded, but Shannon didn't notice.

"How old are they?"

"Brie is twenty-four now and Josh is twenty-seven."

"They were young when your parents died," she said slowly. "Brie must have been only eleven or twelve."

"Yeah, she was eleven."

So he had raised his brother and sister. They had been even younger than she had expected. What a hardship that would have been for a seventeen-year-old boy. No wonder he relished his freedom now. The responsibilities would have been enormous enough for a grown man, but for a boy not even finished high school they must have been almost insurmountable. Her admiration for him rose.

"Tell me more about growing up," she said softly.

"Why?"

"I want to know."

"If you'll tell me about being an Air Force brat."

She nodded and settled in to listen as Jase told her stories about growing up on a ranch, the chores he'd shared with his father. About the endless winters when he and his siblings were housebound and the activities his mother devised to keep three active children happy.

The love and strong family ties that spilled out from his stories intrigued Shannon. She'd always longed for a family, but her father had never remarried, never sought an extended family for them. There had been no grandparents, no aunts, uncles or cousins. She had been so often alone.

Listening to Jase made her think of a family of her own. The one she'd thought to make with Bobby. Both of them were alone in the world before they married. Only her idea of a big family never materialized.

She'd like to think she would love her children as his parents had. She'd want to spend time with them, do things with them, give them lots of love.

When he wound down and began asking her questions about Air Force life, she responded, not realizing how much she gave away by her answers. It was late when they finished talking. The time had flown by and Shannon realized she'd enjoyed every moment.

Thunder rumbled.

"What's that?" She looked outside. It was pitch dark. Rising, she crossed to the back door, peered out into the yard. The wind blew through the trees near the house, their leaves rustling in its strength. Dirt swirled in the yard, looking like fairy dust in the light from the kitchen.

"Was it supposed to storm? I haven't heard a weather forecast in days. Do you think it'll rain? Was that thunder?"

He joined her, scanning the sky. Stars sparkled overhead, but not in the distance.

"Might. Might be a dry storm."

"Heat lightning? I hope not. We could use some rain."

Lightning flashed again in the distance. A few seconds later they heard the rumble of thunder.

Turning, Shannon bumped into Jase. He reached out to steady her and she stood still. She felt closer to him after their dinner conversation. When he lowered his head, she raised hers. Their lips met. He drew her nearer, slowly, as if to give her a chance to pull away.

Shannon stepped closer on her own and pressed her lips to his as dazzling delights spiraled through her.

Slowly she put her arms around him, careful of his ribs, snuggling up against him as his kiss deepened. Her body floated, the kaleidoscope of her emotions scared her. She wanted him, she enjoyed his touch, his hand threaded in her hair, the scent of his skin against hers, the taste of his lips on hers. She was frightened of the depth of emotions he aroused in her.

Jase broke the kiss to sink against her neck, his lips tracing the delicate skin there.

"Ah, Shannon, darlin', what am I going to do with you?" Jase said softly, hugging her close, his face buried against her hair.

She stiffened, wanting to pull away, unable to resist the seduction of being held so tenderly. Slowly, ever so slowly, the raging desire for closer contact eased. He had her locked in his arms, but soon he only held her, giving her a sense of safety and love.

Love?

She pulled away. "I'm tired. I'll do the dishes and then call it a night." She stepped around him and reentered the brightly lit kitchen. Avoiding all contact, she quickly cleared the table and plunged into the soapy water.

Love? No, she would not let herself fall in love with another love 'em and leave 'em cowboy. She had her ranch. One day she'd meet a man who would stay with her. She'd save her love for him.

Love. She refused to grant that name to the feelings she had when she was with Jase. It was only infatuation. Sex appeal. Loneliness. Nothing more.

Shannon tossed and turned after she went to bed, her thoughts turning endlessly to Jase. She remembered every instant they'd been together, every word he'd said, and how he'd said it. Involuntarily she had to smile sometimes. He could be so charming. Even knowing he'd be gone soon didn't make her immune to his charm. Wishing she were stronger, Shannon finally drifted to sleep.

"Shannon." A hand shook her. "Shannon, wake up."

"Jase?" She blinked up, confused. Glancing around she saw it was still dark. The only light spilled in from the hall. "What is it?"

"I think we've got a problem. Come with me."

She sat up. "What time is it?"

"Almost four. Come on, now." His hand grasped her arm and he pulled her up from the bed.

"Wait till I get a robe."

"You don't need it, come on." His hand tugged her across the room and down the hall to the front of the house. Shannon noticed he wore only jeans. What was he doing up?

Standing at the window in the front room, he pointed to a strange orange glow that defined the horizon. "Is that normal?"

She blinked and strained to see better. There was nothing in that direction but open range.

"What is it?"

He sighed, dragging his hand through his hair. "Damn. Unless I miss my guess, it's a fire. I'd kind of hoped you'd tell me something over there always glowed like that in the night. But the smell of smoke is what woke me up."

"Fire! Oh my goodness, Jase, do you think it's a grass fire? That's my range out there. That's where the main herd is grazing."

Panic touched her. Fire. After the dry summer they'd had, the grass had to be as dry as tinder. It would go up like a match. Shannon ran to the front door and yanked it open. The hot wind still blew; now the scent of smoke filled the night air. She closed her eyes, fear overwhelming. She could lose her whole place.

She turned to Jase, but he wasn't there. She heard his voice and hurried into the study.

"Yeah, we'll do what we can from this end. See you." Hanging up the phone, he turned to the door, walking toward his room, speaking as he moved.

"I called the fire department, they'll deploy what they've got and call in the volunteers. We need to get out there and see how bad it is and get those cattle moved."

Shannon crossed to her room, dressing so fast her fingers stumbled on the buttons, all thoughts of a bra gone. Dressed, she dragged her hair back in a ponytail and stomped into her boots. She ran back out to find Jase already in the yard calling Gary and Dink.

"Do we take horses or the truck?" she asked as she ran out. The scent of smoke was strong. The hot air stirred around her. It might be her ranch, but she deferred instinctively to Jase. He knew more about ranching than she did, he'd know what to do.

"I'll take Shadow and cross country the fastest we can go. You take the truck and head for any fencing that will keep the cattle contained. Cut the wires in as many places as you can. I'll try to push the herd away from the flames."

"Won't they go anyway?"

"Honey, cattle are stupid creatures. They'll be so

panic-stricken, they'll stampede. Depending on which way they're heading they could run right into the flames. I'll do my best to head them away, you make sure they have an opening to run through."

Dink, still buttoning his shirt, ran up in time to hear the last of Jase's instructions. "I'll go with you, I can still ride fine. Gary will go with Shannon to help with the wires. Fire department notified?"

"Yeah. They'll be here as soon as they can."

"What happened?"

"Don't know. Heat lightning's my guess."

"How long's it been burning?"

Jase shrugged as he moved to the barn, each movement unhurried, yet swift and competent. "Probably a few hours. We saw lightening before we went to bed."

"Lot of land can burn in a few hours," Dink said, snagging a rope to get his horse.

"Jase?" Shannon paused beside the truck.

"Yeah?"

"Take care of yourself and Shadow." She was afraid for him. Cattle could be so dangerous when spooked.

"Yeah, you too, darlin'. Cut the wires, then get the hell out of the way. When they come, they'll be coming fast."

She nodded. Starting the truck, she backed to the bunkhouse. Gary came flying out and hopped into the truck. As Shannon drove recklessly over the uneven ground, she filled him in on everything she knew.

Seven

"I'm going as close to the fire as I can get, to see what's going on," Shannon told Gary as they bounced across the rough trail. She pushed the truck for all it was worth. Time seemed to drag by, then speed up. She felt disoriented as they hurtled toward the glow that grew brighter and brighter. The smoke started to blur the landscape, thick and gray.

Twice Gary stepped down to open a gate, climbing back into the truck with the gate left wide open. Soon the smoke was so strong, they rolled up the windows to keep it from filling the truck, though they couldn't escape it entirely. Visibility diminished even more. The smoke now seemed to glow orange as it reflected the fire behind it.

The glow grew brighter until she could see the flames licking along in an erratic line, greedily consuming the tall, dry grass. Still a mile or more away when Shannon veered away and drove along the line of fencing of that section, its progress was relentless.

Steers already milled around in panic, bawling and snorting. The scene was chaotic. Scrambling from the cab, Shannon grabbed a pair of wire cutters and attacked the nearest stretch of fence, trying to wrap the loose barbed wire around the posts, moving on to the next one.

Gary hobbled ahead and began cutting the next section. Coughing in the thick air, she ignored discomfort and worked quietly, desperately. Slowly but surely they moved along the fence, destroying all the work that had gone in to stringing the fence in the first place.

Shannon kept a wary eye on the cattle, noting with relief that some of them were drifting her way, taking advantage of the openings and moving away from the encroaching flames. Their panic was abating now that they had a clear path ahead.

She heard thundering hooves and looked around. Jase and Dink rode by, mere silhouettes against the fiery glow. Dawn was still an hour or more away. Shannon returned to work, the need to keep her cattle safe uppermost in her mind. Coughing in the thick smoke, she tried to see the next strand. Her eyes watered almost too much to see.

Afraid to get too far from the truck, she jogged back to it, started it up and moved it ahead. She rejoined Gary, cutting, wrapping the dangerous barbed wire round the posts so cattle wouldn't get caught in it, moving on to the next section of fence. She moved the truck again.

When she heard the thunder, she looked up again. It wasn't caused by lightning this time, but by the sound of cattle as men pushed the steers away from the flames.

"Gary, come on, run. Head for the truck until they've passed."

She ran for the limited safety of the pickup. Gary was only a few steps behind her. In seconds they were surrounded by frantic cattle. The noise was fierce, the confusion rampant. Crazed with fear, the cattle ran blindly. Several bumped into the truck, rocking it. Time and time again Shannon held her breath, wondering if the pickup would protect them as the cattle surged past. Swerving around the truck, the cattle continued their frantic pace.

The line of flames drew steadily closer. Shannon could clearly see Jase and Dink silhouetted in the light of the fire. Her heart caught several times when Jase seemed to head Shadow directly into the flames to try to turn a maddened steer. Each time they turned away unscathed she breathed a sigh of relief.

"Best be moving away from the fire ourselves, Shannon," Gary said as the fire drew close.

She started the engine and turned to the next section. In the distance she could hear the wail of a fire engine, see the flashing lights. Thank God, help at last.

She pulled up a few yards and stopped, her lights flashing to let the firemen know where they were. The fire engine swerved and headed directly for her. In only moments a dozen men jumped out and headed toward the fire to assess the situation. Shannon ran to join them, Jase rode up on Shadow.

"You got here fast," Jase said, dismounting beside the chief.

"We're from a substation near this side of town. The others will be along as soon as they can get here. How long's it been burning?"

"We don't know, but figure a few hours. Depending where it started, it's burned a lot of acreage. The river is over yonder and would have stopped it there."

"Yes, and the highway along the north boundary will stop it eventually. That leaves this area and to the south."

"If it continues in this direction it'll get the house and barns."

"We'll stop it before then, but not much before, unless I miss my guess."

"Can you put it out?" Shannon asked.

"Ma'am, the line looks to be over a couple of miles in length. With this wind, and the grass as dry as it is, it'll take more than what we've got to stop it completely anytime soon. Best to just contain what we can and let it burn itself out. We want to keep your livestock safe, keep your buildings. Beyond that..." He shook his head. "I don't know."

"You have tractors coming?" Jase asked.

"Yes, three. Two from our department, one from one of the local ranchers. As soon as they get here, we'll start to work on the firebreaks."

"Start around the house first," Jase said.

"Right. Then we'll pull in between the cattle and the fire line and do what we can."

"We'll try to bunch the herd, keep it tight and as far from the fire line as we can. We need some more help, though."

"I'll get a horse," Shannon said.

"No. We'll need food, coffee. You do that," Jase said.

"Forget it. This is my place, in case you've forgotten. I'll help defend it." She would not be shunted off like some helpless female.

"God, you're headstrong." He reached out to encircle her neck with his hand, drawing her up for a quick, hard kiss. "Stay away from the fire," he ordered.

"You, too," she said, turning back to the truck.

"Gary, I'm getting a horse, can you stay here and help however they need it?"

He nodded.

"I'll give you a ride back, if you like, ma'am." The fire chief caught up with her. "I need your phone and that'll leave the truck with your man."

"Thanks."

As they drove to the ranch house, two more tanker trucks passed them. Shannon was relieved at the quick response, she only wished they had known about the fire earlier. How much of her range land had been destroyed? Had any cattle been burned?

The first trailer with a tractor pulled into the yard just as they arrived. The fire chief jumped out and went to give directions to the crew while Shannon hurried to the barn to saddle Bugle. She couldn't believe what had happened in the short time since Jase had wakened her. Dawn was beginning to break in the eastern sky. It would help to have light to see what they were doing. How long before the blaze could be extinguished?

Her heart pounded with fear. What would she do if she lost everything. Surely they could protect the house. The fire was still a ways away.

No time to worry about that now. What happened, happened. Now she was anxious to get back to help. She rode out of the yard at a gallop.

The wind blew, fed by the heat of the flames. After a while a fire generated its own wind; how much stronger would it become? She rode toward the fire line. The hot, acrid air burned her lungs, her eyes. She wished she'd remembered to get a bandanna. She used one at branding time, it would help now. But she didn't want to take the time to ride back home to find one.

The cacophony of sound was awful, worse than any roundup she'd attended, worse than the branding and notching she'd worked. The cattle were frantic, milling around, bawling and snorting, thundering first this way then that. It was impossible to contain them with only two men. Even with her help, they wouldn't be able to do much but keep them away from the fire.

The horses whinnied their protest, their hooves rumbling. The snap and spit of the fire, the hoarse shouts of the fire fighters all blended to add to the chaos.

Jase and Shadow worked tirelessly, constantly turning the cattle from the fire line when the steers tried to break toward it in their panic. Shannon joined him and Dink. They needed a dozen men to do the job right. Maybe more would come. She had asked the fire chief to send any volunteers as they arrived. But she didn't have time to think about that now, she had to keep those steers away from the fire. She kicked her horse in front of one recalcitrant animal and headed him back.

The tanker truck had moved to her left, spreading down a line of water in an effort to stop a portion of the fire. With the wind gusting behind them, and the heat of the flames as it consumed the raw grass, it was a futile effort at best.

Where were the dozers? That's what they needed.

Shannon felt the intensity of the heat, heard the crackling as the grass flashed into flame. Her own mount was uneasy and no wonder. Skittish cattle on one hand, a threatening fire behind it, it was a wonder Bugle responded as well as he did.

Time seemed to stand still. Again and again she moved the cattle, again and again breaking left or right to head a recalcitrant steer back. They were moving steadily closer to the house. It seemed as if she played the same scene over and over.

A roar behind her caused her to turn in the saddle. Her truck had been engulfed in flames. For one panicked moment she wondered if Gary were in it. But he would have no reason to be in it. He was working with the firefighters.

Sparing only a brief regret for the loss of her vehicle, she moved closer, crowding the cattle, urging them away from the confusion and danger .

In the distance she saw the tractors. The wide swath they plowed would be the firebreak. They needed to cut a path the entire length for containment. If the fire jumped at any point, they would have the situation all over again.

Smoke blew thicker now, low along the ground, choking everyone. The wind gusted, swirled around, feeding the fire even as the dry grass fed it. Shannon kept rubbing her eyes, they watered in the smoky air, her vision blurred. How much longer would they have to keep it up? The sun shone overhead, its heat exacerbating the fiery air generated by the fire. She had long since given up any hope of knowing what time it was, of wondering if she could get a cold drink somewhere. It felt as if her whole being revolved around driving the cattle away from the fire. She almost couldn't remember doing anything else.

Bugle stumbled. She caught him up. Two steers brushed into him. He stumbled again and she fell over his shoulder, hitting the ground in a numbing jar. Scrambling to her feet, she was relieved to notice that she'd kept the reins in her hand.

"Easy, fellow. We're fine." She patted his neck, trying to calm him. When he took a step, he favored his offside foreleg.

"No! Not now, Bugle. I need you." She ran her hand down his foreleg. There was already swelling near the hoof. She couldn't ride him if he were injured. Two steers ran by, blinded by the smoke, bellowing long and loud.

"Yes, you stupid animals, I feel that way myself." She'd give anything to awaken in her bed and find out this was a nightmare.

Knowing it wasn't, she started for home, leading her injured horse.

Behind her the heat grew more intense, the crackling louder. Glancing over her shoulder, she saw the fire line only yards away. Fear swamped her. Could she outrun it? Could she force her horse to run with them both?

Just then Jase thundered up, bandanna across his nose and mouth, his hat pulled low. He looked like a bandit.

He looked like a knight in shining armor.

"What the hell are you doing? Don't you see how close the fire is?" He leaned over and swept her up before him.

"Bugle's injured. I took a spill. And yes, dammit, I see the fire." Even as she gasped out the words, he headed Shadow away from the fire. They mingled with the cattle, Bugle straining to keep up. Shannon held his reins in a tight grip, not going to lose one of her best horses if she could help it.

"God, Jase, it's awful. I've never lived through anything like this." She wanted to cry, wanted to turn back the clock, wanted the fire to be out!

"Yeah, it's bad. But we've got a lot more men helping now. You take Bugle back to the barn and see to him. They should have the firebreak completed around the house. If we can keep the fire from jumping it, we'll be home-free."

"If I have a home."

"They'll save your home, darlin'. Go on." He dropped her well beyond the fire line. She wanted him to go with her, but before she could say a word, he headed back to the thick of things. With a frustrated sigh, she turned and started walking toward the barn, leading her limping horse.

The last of the fire fighters left just after sundown. The firebreak the tractors plowed held. Deprived of its fuel, the greedy flames gradually died down. The cattle were all contained in sections of the range nearest the house.

Dozens of women and men from neighboring ranches had come to help, with the cattle, the fire fighting, or bringing food to feed the army of workers. Everyone had been fed and sent home.

Shannon was numb, so tired she could scarcely see, too tired to even get up and go to bed. She sat on the back steps, having waved off the last of the volunteers. She was so grateful for the volunteers who had worked hard to save her home.

Would she ever be able to move again?

"Go to bed, darlin'," Jase said, coming in from the barn.

"How are the horses?" she asked listlessly. She should have seen to some of them. Jase was recovering from injuries. Dink and Gary were too old to be doing all they'd done today.

"All doing fine. The vet looked at Bugle, wrapped the leg, gave him something for the swelling. Shadow got a couple of burns, nothing major. The horses the Johnsons used were burned a little, they're fine, too." He sank beside her. They both smelled of smoke.

"Did this destroy the ranch?" she asked, voicing her deepest fear.

"Nope. Might have set you back a bit."

"A bit? I was set back a bit when Rod stole all the money. This is more than a bit."

"From what we can tell, you have most of your herd, you still have your land, once the rains come, the grass will grow."

"Sure, but you know what, Jase? It's been a long time since we've had much rain. Then there's the winter. I have no feed for this herd. Where am I going to get the money to carry me over the winter?"

"My offer as partner still stands," he said slowly.

She sighed and slowly rose. She ached all over. She was so tired she could scarcely breathe and so dirty and smelly she could hardly stand herself.

"I'm going to bed, after I take a long, hot shower."

"Shannon, think on it." Jase stood, as well. He brushed his thumb across one of her cheeks, studying the soot he wiped off.

"I have some insurance, I don't need a partner," she said, turning to go into the house.

Shannon slept twelve hours straight. It was late morning when she awoke. For a long moment she lay in bed, mustering the energy to get up and face all the work needed to recover from the fire.

She'd had a hard time when Bobby left, then died. A hard time when Rod had absconded with her funds.

But this just might be more than she could manage.

Yet the ranch was her responsibility. She had only herself to depend upon.

And Jase.

Could she depend upon him? He had done so much yesterday. He knew what was needed. She could rely on him. She knew it. Yet reliance could be dangerous. She must not learn to depend upon him. They both knew he'd be leaving in a few weeks. She'd learn what she could from him, knowing she had to stand on her own in the end.

There was so much to do, she couldn't afford the luxury of lying in bed.

Two hours later Shannon wished desperately she had stayed in bed. Slowly she replaced the receiver. She felt lost. Totally numb. She didn't have any idea where to turn. Slowly her eyes raised to gaze out the window. She remembered the dreams she'd had when she and Bobby first bought the ranch. How those dreams had slowly changed when he'd left to resume the rodeo circuit.

Her whole life had been tied up in this ranch for the last four years.

Tears welled, spilled over. She couldn't move. She couldn't think. She felt cold deep inside, cold and sick and afraid. What was she going to do?

"Shannon, did you tell Dink to—" Jase came into the study and stopped dead, stunned by the tears coursing down her cheeks.

"Shannon, what's the matter?" He crossed the room in firm strides, going around the desk to her. Leaning over, he brushed away the tears. They kept falling.

"Darlin', what's the matter?" His voice was soft, crooning. He lifted her up and sat in the chair, holding her in his lap.

The tight control Shannon had tried to hold on to broke. Burying her face in his chest, she let the tears fall. All her hard work and efforts were for naught. She was going to lose her ranch.

"He didn't pay the insurance premium," she said finally.

"What?"

"Rod didn't pay the insurance premium. He stole that money, too. I'm not covered for the fire. Oh, Jase, what am I going to do?" Her hand clutched a fistful of his shirt, as if that small reality could hold her together.

"The insurance lapsed?" he asked to clarify.

She nodded, the ache in her heart growing. She felt sick.

"If Rod were here I'd strangle him," she said bitterly.

"You'd have to get in line, darlin'. I'm not feeling too friendly toward the man myself," Jase said, rubbing his good hand across her back, soothing her with his touch.

"How bad is it?" she asked.

Jase had left her a note that morning telling her he'd gone out to inspect the damage with the fire marshal.

"Over sixty percent of the range is burned, including all the land near the river. Water for the cattle is going to be a problem since there isn't any grazing near it."

"Figures, what's one more problem." She didn't want to move. Somehow being held by Jase made the problems seem almost manageable. She'd have to push away soon, but for the time being, she relished being held as if she were cherished.

"And the cattle?" she asked, conscious of his steady heartbeat beneath her fingers. Taking comfort in it.

"We lost about ninety head."

She sat up and stared at him. "No! Ninety?"

He shrugged, tugging her back against his chest. "It could have been worse. Most of them were steers, but a few were calves."

"Do I have any cattle left? After you bought so many, and now I've lost so many, am I still in business?"

"I'll take a proportional share of the loss," he murmured.

"No, I can't let you do that."

"You can't stop me, Shannon. Let's not argue about this now. We've got to start making plans for the next six or eight months. The way I see it, we need to get feed to the section near the river. Then they'll have food and water all in the same area."

"And just who do you think is going to extend me enough credit to get food for all those steers for months on end?"

"Let's think this through logically. You need an extensive influx of capital. Enough to tide you over until next spring at the earliest. Taking out a loan will set you back for even longer."

She sighed and sat up, resting her hands on his shoulders. "So, we're back to the partnership thing, are we?"

He shook his head slowly, his eyes never leaving hers. "Not exactly."

She felt a sense of dread creep over her. Did that mean he was not exactly interested now that there were even more problems on the ranch? It was one thing to offer some ready cash for a short-term need, something else to align himself with a ranch that needed a lot of work to hold it together. The responsibility for bringing it around would be too much for a footloose cowboy more interested in the next town and the next laugh.

"I understand."

"I doubt it. I think we should get married."

She stared at him. "I—did I hear you right? Married?" She was speechless, stunned. It was the farthest thing she had ever expected to hear from him.

Marriage? To Jase?

Her heart began beating heavily in her breast. Mesmerized by the look in his gaze, drawn into the fantasy for a brief blinding instant, she couldn't look away.

"Yeah, you heard right. Marry me, Shannon."

"Why? Jase, marriage is the last thing you want. You'll be leaving in a few weeks. You've kicked over all traces of a responsible life, and you certainly don't want to pick them up here with a ranch that is going to take a lot of work to bring it back in the black."

"I've decided I don't want to be a partner that you can kick out at your whim. I want to try for the nationals, try to be the best I can be. But then I want to come back here when I'm done. Be involved in building up the ranch."

"No. I can't marry you. I can't do that again. I lived like that with Bobby, I won't do it again."

"Where's the problem? You haven't found anyone you're interested in to marry. This way, you can use the money I have saved, get a share of the money I earn in the rodeos."

"And in exchange give up my ranch."

"We'll split it."

She stared at him, longing and hope warring with hard experience of the past. "Sixty-forty?" she asked.

His eyes grew silvery. "I assume I have the forty?"

She nodded thoughtfully. Was she really considering his unorthodox proposal?

"And in return you'll get forty percent of everything I have, as well," he said.

She nodded, knowing she couldn't have forty percent of a cutting horse unless he sold it. But if he wanted to make the deal work both ways, she wouldn't argue.

"Is there a catch to all of this? Why do you want to tie yourself to me? Give up your winnings to build back a ranch you didn't even know existed a month ago?" she asked.

It didn't make any sense. Not with the Jase she thought she knew. Or not with the man she equated with Bobby Blackstone.

Yet Jase had shown on more than one occasion that he was different than Bobby.

He traced his thumb across her lower lip, brushed across again. "Let's just say I want to help and I want a place to come back to when I finish the rodeo. Win or lose, I want a place here."

Love?

There'd been no mention of love.

She wanted to ask him if he felt anything for her beyond the lust that he made no attempt to hide. But it might open up the question of how she felt. And she was afraid to examine that too closely.

"Thank you, Jase, I accept. I'm very grateful that—"

"I don't want gratitude." Anger flared. "I wasn't looking for any and I don't want you to feel that way."

"Okay." She had nothing else to say. She was grateful. But if he didn't want to hear it, she'd keep quiet.

"We'll go into town tomorrow and see about the license," he said.

She licked her lips. Leaning closer, she kissed him.

Touching lightly, she drew back and watched as his eyes darkened. They grew stormy when he was aroused. She smiled slightly and slipped her arms around his neck. Boldly, she leaned against him and opened her mouth against his.

His arms tightened around her and he met her with passion already high. For only a moment Shannon controlled the kiss, but Jase soon commanded. His arms pulled her tightly against him as his tongue plunged in to excite her beyond belief. He deepened the kiss until Shannon lost all awareness of her surroundings. She could only cling to him to keep from spinning away on a cloud of delight.

She leaned closer only to hesitate when he groaned slightly when she pressed his ribs. Sitting up, she pulled away and looked at him in concern. "Are you all right?"

"Fine." He kissed her lightly, his tongue just skimming across her lips.

"Tomorrow we'll see the doctor again about your ribs, you could have damaged them further yesterday. In fact, I don't know how you did all you did."

She clung to the mundane to keep her head on an even keel. The sensations that shot through her had nothing to do with evenness.

"See what a good wife you'll make," he said mockingly as he kissed her one last time. Then he set her up on her feet. "There's work to be done."

She nodded, suddenly worried about the turn her life had taken. Had she really committed to marry another rodeo cowboy?

Had she set herself up for another heartache?

Eight

"This is insane," Shannon grumbled as she crossed her arms over her chest and glared at Jase the next morning as he drove them into Tumbleweed. With stops planned at the courthouse, the hospital, and the feed store, they'd gotten an early start.

Not that it mattered to Shannon. She had scarcely slept two hours all night. She'd been too hasty in accepting his offer of marriage. Now that she'd had time to think—

He glanced at her, then back at the road. "What's insane?"

"Us getting married. I don't want to get married."

"You're calling it off?" He raised an eyebrow, but his voice remained level, unconcerned.

"There must be some other way."

"Lots of other ways. Most of them involving loans which you are adamantly against."

"Why can't you be my partner?"

"I will be, partner, husband, lover."

She stared, dumbfounded. "*Lover?*" she squeaked.

Jase shrugged. "There's no denying the attraction between us, is there? Given time, we're bound to give in to it. And once married, you won't have all those inhibitions."

"They aren't inhibitions, they're principles! I never agreed to be your lover," she hissed, incensed. Was that all he wanted? Was marriage just a way to get her into his bed?

"But you did agree to become my wife," he said smoothly.

She frowned at him and turned to look out the window. This made matters even worse than before. Her heart skipped a beat then began racing.

Lovers. He planned for them to become lovers.

"Do you think getting married gives you the right to just hop in my bed whenever you feel like it?" she asked, still scowling out the window.

"No. But one day you'll invite me in and then I'll feel I have the right."

"Fat chance." She was silent for a while, then slid a glance his way. "Is that why you want marriage?"

"One of the reasons."

"What are the others?"

"We went over this yesterday."

"Humor me. Yesterday I was still in shock about the lack of insurance. Now I've had time to think this over and—"

"And time to panic about the marriage, so you want out. Why? You've said you haven't found anyone else you want to marry. You can use my knowledge about ranching. You sure as hell need the money I can bring into this. And my touch doesn't disgust you."

On the contrary, she thought wryly, it delighted her.

She was getting so she almost craved his casual touches. Squirming slightly, she shifted away from him, afraid he might read her mind.

She'd loved Bobby. And their marriage had been a disaster. How would she and Jase ever manage a marriage where neither loved the other?

"So what do you get out of it, besides half my ranch?" she asked sulkily.

"Forty percent, remember? Do you want to go by a lawyer and write up a prenuptial agreement?"

She shook her head. She trusted Jase.

Stunned, she held her breath.

She trusted him!

Why? He embraced the same life-style as Bobby. She'd accused him time and time again of shirking responsibility. Yet he hadn't let her down once. She trusted he would always stand by his word.

"No. I don't need an agreement. What else?"

"I get the opportunity to build up a spread that has a tremendous potential. Get to see it from the beginning, so to speak. And sooner or later, I get you."

Sooner or later…he was probably right. She swallowed. Unless she did something to protect herself, she was afraid she was in for a heart load of trouble.

"That's not part of the agreement."

"I can wait."

"It won't be for long, you're leaving in a couple of weeks, aren't you?" She held her breath. Would their marriage keep him at the ranch?

"Yeah, soon as I get the word from the doctor. Will you come to Las Vegas to see me compete in the finals?"

"Pretty sure of yourself, aren't you? You've missed a lot of rodeos."

"I know and I'll have to work like hell to make up the points. But Shadow's better than ever. That competition is my best bet. I'll see where I stand in the bronc riding, but may have to bow out of that this year."

Disappointment flashed through her. She'd known he was leaving, but something deep inside had hoped he'd stay once he'd mentioned marriage.

Yet why should he? He had the best of all worlds, just like Bobby. A wife and ranch waiting while he enjoyed all the excitement and pleasures of the rodeo circuit. And she'd be left behind again, lonely and alone.

"So will you come if I make the finals?" he repeated.

"Sure, might cramp your style, though, having your wife show up."

He chuckled, shaking his head. "Don't you worry about that, darlin', just come and root for me."

Jase pulled the truck into the parking slot before the courthouse and cut the engine. Shannon stared at the stone building as if she'd never seen it before. Butterflies danced in her stomach, she felt shaky, almost sick.

She couldn't go through with this. Who was she trying to kid? She'd have to tell Jase she'd changed her mind. If he didn't want to be her partner, she'd get a loan. She'd made it so far on her own, this was no time to change that.

"Shannon?" His hand came around behind her neck, beneath the braid. He gently massaged the tight muscles. "Darlin', it'll be okay. We'll do just fine. Trust me on this, all right?"

She glanced over at him, wishing she could believe him, but too afraid of heartache.

When he leaned over to kiss her, she wanted to melt into his embrace, forget about problems and decisions and the future. Give in to the longing to make the world be a kind place, a happy place, not a place of sadness and loneliness.

But she refrained, pushing against him.

"If we're going in, let's go before I change my mind," she said, refusing to meet his eyes lest he see the longing in hers. Tilting her chin, she pushed open her door and climbed down into the warm morning air.

It took less than ten minutes to get the license. When they were again in the truck, this time heading for the hospital, Jase spoke evenly, "Tell me about your first wedding."

"We got married by a justice of the peace in Austin. My friend Cathy and her brother were the only ones there."

"Did you have a pretty white dress?"

"No. Bobby was in a hurry. There wasn't time."

That should have been her first clue to how that marriage would work. Bobby hadn't wanted to wait for anything. It had been a hurried affair, not that she had had any reason to want anything different. Her family was all gone, she had few friends to worry about attending. Cathy and her brother had made it as festive as possible given the circumstances.

"Do you belong to a church here in Tumbleweed?"

"What? Yes. Why, do you want to be married in a church?" She stared at him, startled. She had never thought about the ceremony. She'd assumed they'd just have the local justice of the peace perform it.

"Yeah I do. Will you have a problem with that?" He threw her a quick look.

"I guess not. Only…"

"Only what?"

"Maybe we need to discuss this. What exactly are you planning on for a wedding?"

He shrugged. "I haven't thought it through in any detail. I guess I figured you'd want to have it in a church. Gary or Dink would love to walk you down the aisle, they're both crazy about you. I'd like to see my bride in white."

"Jase, I can't. I'm hardly a virgin. I was married for eighteen months."

"Cream colored, then. A pretty dress. Maybe a veil or fancy hat."

For a moment she daydreamed about a dress that would knock his socks off, make her as beautiful as brides were supposed to be on their wedding day. She wanted to feel the glow being in love was supposed to bring.

It was nothing but wishful thinking. She was much too practical. There was no love here and she wasn't going to pretend there was.

"Jase, this is my second marriage."

"So? This is my only one, darlin'"

Only one?

"I don't know, getting married in a church makes it seem so…so permanent, somehow."

"It is permanent, Shannon. What did you think we

were doing, getting married for a year or so, then go our separate ways?" There was a hard edge to his voice, an angry glint in his eyes.

She nodded. Bobby had been disenchanted within a few months. She couldn't expect Jase to last any longer.

"I don't operate that way. Once we're married, we'll stay married."

The silence that filled the truck could almost be touched, she thought as they drove to the hospital. Jase didn't speak again and she was afraid to open her mouth. Nothing was going as she had thought. Not once had she expected him to want to keep to their marriage once the ranch was in the black.

And she couldn't picture herself being tied to a husband who rarely stayed home, who preferred the carefree life of a rodeo rider to the responsibilities of a respectable rancher a second time. How could she stand to know her husband sought the women who flocked to rodeos for the vicarious thrills the cowboys provided even though they had no other commitment between them?

"Are you coming in with me?" Jase asked.

She blinked and looked around. They were in the hospital parking lot.

"You don't need me."

She wanted some time to think this through. It still wasn't too late to change her mind, to come up with an alternative.

"A man likes his family around him at a time like this. Come hold my hand."

She flashed him a look. "We're not married yet."

"But we will be, won't we?" His gaze was rock steady, his eyes locked onto hers.

Something melted deep within, something began to bloom. Was it hope for a better future? Slowly, Shannon nodded her head. "Yes, we will be."

"Good, come with me."

Jase laced his fingers through hers as they walked into the county hospital. Shannon tightened her fingers around his, hoping she wasn't making a huge mistake. She felt as if she were on the edge of a dark precipice, one step wrong and she'd plunge over into the dark unknown.

How much was she influenced by the attraction that blossomed between them? His touch sent shimmering tingles up her arm. His arrogant, confident stride brought pride that such a man would be interested in her. He could look anywhere for a wife, find someone who could bring him a willingness to explore the future together even if he did prefer rodeos to ranching.

Instead, he'd picked her. He agreed to help her build up the Bar Seven in exchange for forty percent. And in return he promised to give her forty percent of everything he owned, from Shadow to future earnings.

Shown a waiting room in the out-patient department, they sat to await the doctor.

"How do you feel?" the physician asked Jase as he removed the ace bandages twenty minutes later.

True to his word, Jase had insisted Shannon accompany him into the cubicle and hold his hand. His grip tightened, threatening to crush her bones, but she remained silent, knowing he must hurt much worse than he was letting on if he needed to hold on so tightly.

"Like I fell off a horse and cracked my ribs," Jase said easily as the doctor probed his still discolored flesh. Wincing once, he flicked a glance at Shannon.

She bit her lower lip, upset he was still in pain. She wanted to slap the doctor's hands away and soothe the bruised areas. Bringing his clasped hand up she cradled it between her breasts, longing to give him some comfort.

"You're a lucky man. Fighting that fire didn't seem to set you back."

"How did you know about that?" Shannon asked, surprised.

"Talked to one of the fire fighters brought in for smoke inhalation. Told me about the blaze, and how this man did more to keep things under control than anyone."

Shannon nodded, tightening her grip. Jase would always be like that. Why did she continue to think he avoided responsibility? He made sure things got done. He only refused to acknowledge it.

"How long before I can compete?" Jase asked, shrugging back into his shirt. Without regard for Shannon's sensibilities, he unzipped his jeans and thrust the shirt in. She glanced down involuntarily. Try as she might, she could not keep her eyes off that taut belly, the drift of hair that was cut off by the white band of his briefs. The rasp of the zipper as he snapped it up brought her gaze back to his face. His eyes watched her, dark and glowing. He knew.

"Not before that cast comes off. I doubt if they'd let you compete with it, anyway. No use telling you to take it easy for a few more months, is there?"

Jase smiled and shook his head. "I've a date in Las Vegas come December."

"Okay, cowboy, good luck." The doctor shook his hand and left.

"We've two more stops before we head home. Want to grab a bite of lunch first?" Jase asked as he put his hat on and took Shannon's hand.

"Two more stops? I thought we just had to go to the feed store to arrange for hay."

"And to a dress shop to find your wedding gown."

"Jase—"

He swung her around, cupping her face in his hands, the hard ridge of the cast scratchy against her right cheek, his fingers gentle.

"Listen, Shannon, I want to see my bride dressed like one. I want this wedding to be as traditional as we can get it in two weeks. We'll stop by your church on the way back to the ranch and talk to the minister."

"Two weeks?"

"That's all the time I can give you to plan it."

"Is that all the time you'll be here?" she asked.

"No, I'll stay a week after that. Once the cast is off, I have to go, you know that. You've always known that."

She nodded. Knowing it didn't make it easier.

Lowering his head, Jase kissed her gently. His lips moving persuasively across hers. He made no effort to deepen the kiss, but pulled back after a moment to stare down into her smoky blue eyes.

"I'll be back for Thanksgiving."

"And the finals?"

"You said you'd come to them. We'll go together, they're right after Thanksgiving."

She nodded, wondering if he'd return for her, or would he call with an excuse and stay on the circuit to enjoy the parties the cowboys always threw on any excuse.

The dress she found was wonderful, soft and romantic and elegant. It made her feel more feminine than at any point in her life. Fitting her like it had been made for her, the snug bodice flowing into a sassy short skirt. The lacey soft edges of the long sleeves scalloped her wrists. With it she paired a storybook hat. With her dark hair, the soft off-white color brought a faint pink tinge to her cheeks, a warm honey glow to her tan. Her eyes seemed bluer, her features glowed. She stared at herself for a long time in the mirror. Would Jase like it?

"It is perfect, madam. He'll always remember your wedding day," the salesclerk said as she swished a fold, straightened the sleeve.

"I guess. It doesn't look much like me."

Shannon hesitated. Gone was the tough woman who had tried to make a go of a cattle ranch. Gone was the lonely girl who had been dragged from air base to air base. Gone was the unhappy wife and widow. In her place stood an alluring woman, wrapped in a feminine mystique. Slowly she smiled, unexpected sensations seeping throughout.

"I'll take it." She tilted her head, picturing herself walking down the aisle. Picturing Jase as he waited by the minister. Her heartbeat increased. Color rose in her cheeks.

"Well?" Jase asked some moments later when she joined him in the main floor of the dress shop. He looked disappointed. "You didn't find anything?"

"Yes. I found a dress. The clerk's wrapping it."

"I want to see it."

"Not until the wedding. It's bad luck, you know."

He frowned. "Did you get something pretty?" he asked suspiciously, his hand sweeping back a strand of hair from her cheek, lingering a moment.

"Yes, I think it's pretty. You can tell me, after we're married."

"Ah, like that, is it?" he teased.

She nodded, happiness welling up. Maybe they could work something out.

The visit to the feed store proved a nightmare. Shannon watched as Jase and the owner negotiated feed deliveries, appalled at the amount of money involved. She grew quieter and quieter as the magnitude of what she'd owe Jase became clearer. He must have a lot of money saved from winnings to be able to agree to the terms. Though he drove a hard bargain, the amount of feed needed to carry them through the winter was astonishing.

"Jase," she said as they walked back to the truck. "Maybe we ought to sell more of the herd, wait until next spring and buy then. That would save all this money. It's too much."

"Let me worry about that now, darlin'," he said, opening the door for her.

When he climbed in, she turned to him. "Don't patronize me, Jase, or treat me like a child. None of that 'there, there, dear, don't worry your pretty little head about things.' This is *my* ranch. And I'm running it. I asked for some help to teach me how, not for you to take over. I still have sixty percent ownership don't forget."

"How could I when you bring it up all the time? Fine, what do you want to do? I told you before when you wanted to sell cattle now is not the time to do it. If you sell at a loss now, how will you have any money to buy in the spring? I have the money for the feed. Consider it my input to the ranch, to justify the forty percent."

"I thought marrying me got you the forty percent."

"Dammit, Shannon, let it drop." He rammed the truck into gear and left the feed lot with gravel spinning and dust rising.

"I'll pay you back," she said.

"How does a wife pay back her husband? Our assets will be mingled."

"Well, if we ever get a divorce, I'll—"

"Stop right there!" He pulled to the side of the road and slammed on the brakes. "If you're thinking of going into this marriage with the intention of getting a divorce, change your thought process."

"No, I—"

"I told you it is for good. If you can't handle that, decide now. Once we're married, we stay married."

She was silent. She was not consciously thinking about a divorce in the future. But would Jase feel constrained in a marriage? Would he one day want to regain the freedom he so blithely traded away?

She felt so obligated, as if she were gaining

everything while he gained nothing. She didn't like the feeling. She wanted to be independent, able to stand on her own, or at the very least to be an equal partner.

"I'll sleep with you, then," she blurted. At least he'd get something from the marriage.

"Dammit to hell, Shannon! You think prostituting yourself for your ranch is going to make me feel good?" he growled out. His hands gripped the wheel so tightly his knuckles showed white. His jaw clenched furiously as he tried to control his anger.

"I'm just trying to give you something in exchange for all you're doing. I love this ranch, Jase, and you're making it possible for me to keep it. To remain on it. I'm grateful—"

"I don't want your damn gratitude. I don't want you in my bed because you're grateful, or you think of it as payment for the few lousy dollars I'm putting in. When you come to my bed I want you there because you want me as much as I want you. No other reason."

She shivered. He was flaming angry. She swallowed and tried to think of something else to say. She hadn't meant to make him so mad. Watching him warily, she realized her mistake. It had sounded as if she agreed to share his bed as some kind of payment when in fact she'd been trying to hold up her end of the deal.

I want you in my bed because you want me as much as I want you.

She closed her eyes as a delicious warmth skimmed over her.

He wanted her, he'd made that clear more than once. He'd been frank and up front. And if she were equally frank, she'd admit she wanted him, as well. Wanted to explore the excitement he generated, see what the two of them together could create.

Would it be wild and hot and frenzied, or slow and languid and deep? Would they burn out fast or glow endlessly?

Would he tire of her? Closing her eyes, Shannon refused to dwell on any of the choices. She'd just blown it. He wouldn't listen to anything she said right now.

And she was too afraid to admit she wanted him. To do so would be to admit the crack in the ice around her heart, to admit to the possibility that she would end up feeling more for Jase than she had for anyone before. And that would open herself up to the possibility of incredible hurt if he cheated like Bobby had or ignored her.

She wasn't ready to do that.

It was late afternoon when they reached the ranch. Shannon kept her expression neutral, though she almost giggled inside at the remembered expression on the minister's face when Jase told him they wanted to be married. Anyone less lover-like than Jase would have been hard to find.

He planned the wedding in a totally businesslike manner. He scowled when Shannon said anything, was abrupt and curt. She knew he was still angry with her, but she couldn't help finding the humor in the situation. Knowing her very life would probably be in danger if she gave way to the laughter that threatened, she concentrated on keeping a straight face.

"I'll do the chores," she said as he pulled the truck

to a stop near the house. Hopping down, her smile couldn't be contained.

"Fine. I'll call my family and let them know the good news," Jase replied, slamming his door.

His family. She hadn't thought of them once.

More and more this took on the sense of a true wedding, a true marriage.

Shannon forked down the hay, scooped the grain, all by rote. Her thoughts churned. She was committed to marriage. To a man who planned to leave a week after the wedding and would be gone longer than she'd known him before he'd come back.

She didn't want him to go. Or if he went, she wanted him to take her with him. She'd miss him desperately when he left—from his lopsided smile, to the touch of his fingers against her cheek; from his arrogant confident stride, to his kindness to the old cowboys who worked her ranch. His touch ignited her. His teasing warmed her. His ability around horses and cattle enthralled her. There was nothing about him she'd change.

Except…maybe his sense of responsibility.

Yet he was who he was. He wasn't perfect. He had a temper, he was bossy on occasion, and he always thought he knew best. And sometimes he was right.

What was she going to do? How could she marry him, live with him through the years? How could she bear to be apart from him?

Even now she wanted to rush into the house and see what he was doing. Hear his lazy drawl as he talked on the phone. Feel the tingle from his fingers as he brushed past her when setting the table. Taste the essence of him in a kiss.

Slowly, Shannon turned and finished the chores. Time enough to see him when she finished her tasks. After all, they were going to be married soon. He'd live with her in every sense after that.

Nine

When Shannon returned to the house, she met Jase leaving. He had his duffel bag under one arm, his second set of boots in his hand.

"Where are you going?" she asked. He wasn't leaving, was he? Had she made him so angry he was cutting out?

"To the bunkhouse," he said, stepping around her, walking firmly toward the building.

"Why?" She spun around and hurried to keep up with him.

"Why do you think, Shannon? To protect your reputation, of course."

"That's dumb. You've been staying in the house for weeks now."

"But we weren't engaged before." He continued walking.

She stopped dead.

Engaged.

Slowly, a soft smile tilted her lips. They were engaged. She hadn't been engaged before. A feeling of delight slowly grew, warming her, enchanting her. For two weeks she'd be engaged.

"Wait." She ran to catch up, reaching out to grasp his arm. "It doesn't change anything."

He dumped his duffel and boots and swung around to draw her up against him, resting his head on her hair. "The hell it doesn't. After your generous offer this afternoon, how could I refuse? How could I keep my hands to myself until we're married if we're living together?"

"Sarcasm doesn't become a newly engaged man," she chided gently at his tone when referring to her offer. Embarrassed that he'd thought she'd offer it in exchange for the money, she wanted to keep her face tight against his chest, negating the need to look at him.

"Yeah, well we have a lot to do the next few weeks. And I need to get my rest. What kind of nights do you think I have listening to you slide the clothes off your body? How much sleep do you think I get imagining you naked between the sheets? Listening to you toss and turn in bed every night until it's all I can do to refrain from knocking down your door and finding out why you can't sleep."

She leaned against him as her legs grew weak. She could feel the raw need in him, trembled at the depth of his feelings. If only she wasn't so afraid to let go.

He tilted back her head until he could gaze down into her eyes. The soft afternoon air swirled by like a caress against her skin. "Cowboys are a rowdy bunch. I don't want to give cause for speculation and gossip about you. I'll bunk in with Dink and Gary until the wedding."

For one splendid moment Shannon felt cherished. No one had ever taken such care for her before. Jase made her feel special, treasured.

"Okay, I guess. But you'll still eat with me?"

When he hesitated, she tightened her grip. "Please. It's not as much fun to cook for one as for two."

It wasn't as much fun to eat alone anymore, either. She'd have enough solitary meals when he left.

"All right. Go start dinner, I'll be up in a little while."

He released her and picked up his things. Without another glance in her direction he headed for the bunkhouse.

He still simmered from her words this afternoon. That wasn't the reason he was moving. He did want to protect her. She was right, her reasons for not hopping into bed with him were her principles. He admired her for that, even when he thought some times that she wanted him as much as he wanted her.

He pushed open the door to the bunk house. The large living area held several comfortable sofas and coffee tables, scarred by years of boots. Gary was in the kitchen and looked over at Jase.

"You two have a fight?" he asked.

"No. Just seemed the thing to do. Don't want to cause gossip."

Gary shrugged. "No one outside the ranch knows what the sleeping arrangements are, and Dink and I sure ain't talking."

"Shannon and I are getting married in a couple of weeks."

He didn't expect the wide grin on Gary's face.

"Well, hot damn, about time. Glad to hear it."

"You and Dink can draw straws to see who walks

her down the aisle." Jase said, heading for the hall and looking for an empty room.

"Married in a church?" Gary called after him.

"Yes, in two weeks."

"Wait until Dink hears this," Gary mumbled, turning back to the stove.

Jase dumped his duffel on the bed and went in search of sheets and blankets.

He made the bed then stretched out on it. There were chores to do. Dinner to get through. But he wanted a moment to think

Since he'd proposed his cockamamie idea, he'd refused to admit why he suggested such a thing. He thought back to the nights he'd sat up playing with the numbers, trying to see how he and his brother and sister would make it through to spring. They had not had the setback of burned fields. He remembered feeling overwhelmed and scared. If he couldn't make it work, they would go to foster care, he'd lose the ranch, and who knew what would happen to them.

But he'd made it work. And then walked away when Brianna graduated from college.

Neither of the other two wanted to run the place, and he wanted time to try the rodeo, so he installed a manager.

Feeling free for the first time since his folks had died, he'd loved the rodeo. He loved challenging himself against 1500 pounds of raw energy. He liked the smooth precision of Shadow, the satisfaction when they placed first. The knowledge he'd trained the horse and it was paying off.

So why change all that for a ranch that was perilously close to needing the same kind of devotion his had back in the day? Why tie himself to a woman he couldn't be sure would ever fully accept him.

Maybe he'd hit his head harder than he thought when he'd been bucked off that bronc.

Jase worked tirelessly for the next two weeks. Shannon learned more than she had ever imagined about ranching, from interviewing and hiring new hands, to recovery from a fire. Jase arranged removal of the carcasses and the burned-out shell of her truck. She went into town and bought a new one, courtesy of her fiancé.

The two new cowboys were immediately sent to work on repairing the fences, while Jase worked out a plan with Shannon for rotating the cattle on the fields the fire had missed and spreading enough feed to continue the growth of the cattle on the burned areas. He arranged for water tankers to deliver water to troughs on the fields cut off from water. He showed her how to estimate the next order and make sure the feed store delivered it on time and dumped it where she wanted it.

He reviewed maintenance procedures, accounting procedures, and emergency planning. She felt as if she were in school again and cramming for a final exam.

And never once in the fourteen days did Jase touch her.

Shannon wasn't sure at first. Then she began to watch for it.

He avoided all contact. He continued to tease her, his smile would still speed up her heart rate. His normally easy-going attitude was evident, but something else shimmered there, as well. She wondered what it was—and could only come up with a smoldering anger.

He was still mad at her for offering to sleep with him. And she didn't know how to change that anger. She wanted to let him know that she wanted him as much as he wanted her, but couldn't just blurt it out. If he gave any indication that he wanted more from her, she'd respond in an instant. But he was aloof, distant. He told her all she needed to learn, then left to practice with Shadow.

Even their meals together were few and far between.

When the new ranch hands moved in, Jase said it would be beneficial if he ate with them, giving them information about the ranch they'd need in their jobs.

It sounded reasonable, only Shannon missed him more than she'd have thought possible.

She began to count the days until the wedding. Knowing that from that day he'd have to eat with her, whether he wanted to or not, or cause talk. And he'd been very careful to make sure there was no gossip. She counted on that attitude lasting after the wedding.

The day before the wedding, Jase went into town. Shannon didn't know he'd gone until she went looking for him in the late afternoon.

"Gone to Tumbleweed," Tony Rogers, one of the new hands, explained when she questioned as to Jase's whereabouts.

"When will he be back?" she asked.

"Don't know. Tomorrow, I'm sure. Probably wanted one last fling." He grinned and winked.

She smiled and turned away, annoyed that Jase had gone without telling her. Maybe she would have wanted something from town. He could have asked.

When he didn't return by supper, she began to get worried.

When she finally went to bed and his truck still hadn't turned into the yard, she grew angry. Who did he think he was to stay out all night the eve of his wedding? Was he at some bachelor party? Drinking and partying up a storm on his last night as a free man without telling her anything about it? Didn't he care that she was worried sick?

She swallowed the tears that threatened. He was a free man. They weren't married yet.

But sleep proved elusive. She strained to hear the pickup when it returned. Instead she heard the tick of the clock in the hall, the chimes announcing the hour. One. Two. Three.

Awaking early, Shannon lay in bed wondering if Jase had ever returned. Had he changed his mind and just taken off? They had a wedding scheduled today. Surely he'd tell her if he was calling it off.

She tried to picture herself married again. Tried to guess about their future, wondered if she were making a mistake, or the best decision ever. One thing for certain, she had never pictured herself marrying a drifting rodeo cowboy again. Would she ever reconcile herself to their basic differences? Would it make a difference down the road? She wished she could see into the future.

"You look pretty as a picture," Gary said later that morning as Shannon opened the kitchen door at his knock. "Right proud you asked me to walk you down the aisle, missy."

She smiled uncertainly. "Thank you again for agreeing. Did everyone else leave?" She'd heard the cars and trucks earlier, then only silence.

"Sure did. Wanted good seats. Ready?"

She nodded, smoothing her hands nervously over her skirt. She wished she could take one last look in the mirror, but that would only delay her leaving. She'd double checked everything already.

She'd done her hair up, with soft tendrils drifting down beside her face. Her hat framed her face, lending an air of fragile beauty. Her dress was perfect. If only she wasn't so nervous.

She didn't talk on the ride to the church, but Gary made up for it.

"Sure a fine day for a wedding, don't you think?" Without waiting for her response, he continued. "The boys are excited about seeing their boss married. They all like Jase. That Tony knew him from the rodeos. We'll miss him while he's gone. You going with him?"

She shook her head.

"Good thing, we need someone here to run the place. Not that Dink and I couldn't do it for you. For a week or so anyway. You think on that if you want to go off and watch your man ride."

Her man.

She twisted her fingers together. She'd see him in the finals, if he got that far. She'd seen him in Fort Worth, but only to watch him fall, be injured. She'd seen him on Shadow. He couldn't get much better than that. She didn't need the rodeo arenas to know how good he was.

The small church parking lot was crowded with cars and trucks when they drew up. Shannon noted with relief that Jase's pickup truck was parked near the door. At least he'd shown up. Had he ever returned to the ranch last night?

"Ready?" Gary asked.

"As I'll ever be," she murmured, taking a deep breath.

Shannon had asked her friend Cathy to stand up with her, and Cathy now waited at the steps, dressed in a soft rosy dress.

She gave Shannon a hug.

"Oh, honey, your groom is like totally fabulous. No wonder you're getting married again. I'm so glad. You're going to be so happy."

"Maybe. I'm glad to see you. Thanks for coming on such short notice."

"Hey, it wouldn't be your wedding without me, would it?"

Shannon grinned at her. "I hope this is the last time."

"Me too, that hunk is too gorgeous. I need to get over to see you more often, look at all I missed."

Shannon had neglected her friend lately. Cathy still worked at the bank west of Tumbleweed and Shannon had been so caught up with the problems caused by Rod she'd not kept up with Cathy as she should have.

"Here." Cathy reached over the bench and picked up

a bouquet of white roses and baby's breath. The fragrance wafted around them.

"They're so pretty, thank you."

"Jase got them for you," Cathy said, "and asked me to be sure you got them before we go inside."

Touched, tears threatened. Shannon blinked and drew in a shaky breath. "Is it time?"

"If you're ready, I'll wave at the pianist and we'll start."

Shannon nodded, dipped to smell the bouquet, then smiled at Gary, linking her left hand through his arm, her right holding the bouquet so all could see. Pinning a bright smile on her face, she entered the church. She was getting married.

As she glided down the aisle Shannon saw no one and nothing but the tall, golden man waiting at the altar. He was wearing a dark gray suit, the attire looking totally foreign on him. Yet he looked incredible. Her eyes locked with his and her heart soared.

She'd give anything if this marriage would work. Maybe in time they would grow close. Maybe in time he'd grow to love her. Maybe—

Jase reached out to claim her hand almost before Gary stopped. His hand was warm and firm, his fingers tightening slightly, then relaxing as they turned together to face the minister.

Shannon said her vows in a firm voice, wondering if everyone could see her heart pounding so hard it almost shook her. She was committed and would do all she could to make the marriage work.

Jase's vows were equally strong, his low, husky voice

ringing out in the church.

When the minister pronounced them man and wife, Shannon's heart skipped a beat. Jase turned her and cupped her face in his hands.

"You are the most beautiful bride I ever saw," he said before he lowered his mouth to hers.

It wasn't a brief, chaste kiss, but powerful and deep and long. His lips coaxed an instant response from hers. His tongue courted hers, mating in a ritual as old as humankind.

The whistles and stamping of the cowboys shattered the moment and Shannon blushed fiercely as Jase's eyes danced in amusement. Waving casually to the cat-calling men, he turned her to face the congregation. It was only then that Shannon realized how many people had come to the event. The church was full. Tears filled her eyes. She hadn't known all her neighbors would attend.

The reception was loud and boisterous and plain fun. Jase introduced her to his brother, who had stood as best man. "Brie couldn't make it," Josh said, holding Shannon's hand longer than Jase liked. With a smug smile at his older brother, he kissed her palm and released her.

"She sends her best and wants to meet you as soon as she can. We never expected Jase to fall."

"Fall?" Shannon slid her glance to her husband.

"Yeah, into the clutches of a mere woman," he teased as Jase captured her hand lest Josh take it again.

"Well, if that's the way you feel—"

"Now, now, no fighting until the honeymoon's over," Josh said, laughing at Shannon's indignant expression.

Jase glanced at her, then his brother. "We're not taking a honeymoon exactly. At least not right now. There's a lot to do around the ranch."

"Surely you can take a week off," Josh said.

"Maybe later. I want Shannon to come to Las Vegas for the finals."

"Still working on that?"

"Sure. This arm set me back, but I was far enough ahead in a couple of events that I still have a chance. I just need to ride enough between now and then to accumulate the needed points."

"The others in contention aren't going to sit back and make it easy," Josh commented.

"Yeah, I know. That's why as soon as I can ride, I'm hitting every rodeo I can make."

"What do you think about this, Shannon?" Josh asked.

"She doesn't like rodeo cowboys," Jase said easily.

Josh looked at his brother, then his new sister-in-law. "How'd she tangle up with you then?"

She wondered the same thing herself.

"Just fate." Jase threaded his fingers through hers and tugged gently. "Want some more champagne?"

She nodded and smiled.

She enjoyed the party her friends and neighbors had planned. Time enough for doubts after they returned home.

It was late when they drove back to the ranch. Some of the cowhands had left earlier to take care of chores. What a change, Shannon thought. For so long she'd been the one to take care of everything, to worry about everything. Now she could share that burden with someone else, at least for the next week or so. Then it would all fall to her again.

But for the time being she enjoyed the luxury of not having to worry about every detail. Knowing that all the chores would get done on time even if she were absent from the ranch, eased some of the burden she'd carried for so long.

She was so grateful to Jase. Her heart filled with gratitude and she wished she could share it with him. But he didn't want gratitude. And she wasn't making that mistake again.

"It's been a long day. You tired?" he asked as he pulled up by the front door.

"No. We could go 'round to the back."

"Not dressed like you are, darlin'. You look sensational."

"Thank you for my bouquet. It's beautiful. I didn't expect it," she said, touching the blossoms lightly. She had tossed it at the party, but Annie Simms, who had caught it, had returned it, claiming Shannon would want to hold on to it. Then Annie had left with a most determined look in her eye.

"I don't think you expect much of anything, darlin'. Did you like your wedding?"

"It was very special. I felt special," she said shyly, her eyes on her fingers, on the delicate rose petals. "I think every woman dreams of a wedding that she'll remember all her life. A wonderful time of happiness and sharing that with friends and neighbors. I had that today. It was perfect."

"Good." He opened the door and came around to open hers. Helping her from the truck, they walked up the shallow steps to the porch. Opening the door, Jase turned and swept her up into his arms, stepping boldly across the threshold.

Shannon grinned in delight. Flinging one arm around his neck to keep from falling, she brought her face close to his. "Another tradition you don't want to miss?" she whispered.

"Right."

When he made to set her down, she tightened her arm. "We can go to bed now if you like," she said brazenly.

He hesitated, then continued lowering her until she stood on her own feet. Keeping one arm around her shoulders, he asked her, "Why?"

She swallowed. She hadn't expected to be questioned. She thought he'd just storm down the hall and be glad she'd agreed.

"I thought you wanted—I mean, we're married now and all."

"Yes, married and all." He caught her chin between his thumb and fingers, tilting her up until she had to face him. "What changed in the last two weeks?"

She couldn't speak. She couldn't say anything. Her eyes spoke for her, anguished, afraid, yearning. She wanted him as he wanted her to want him, but she couldn't say a word.

"Go to bed, Shannon, I'll see you in the morning." He released her and strode by, going through the kitchen and out the back door, the screen slamming behind him.

She stood stock still, shame and humiliation trickling through every cell in her body. He didn't want her after all.

Or not enough to take what she so freely offered. Feeling splintered, she turned and headed slowly to her room. The glow of the day faded as she faced a lonely wedding night.

Confused and hurt, Shannon slowly studied her reflection in the mirror as she drew the hat from her head. She had looked pretty. Jase had thought so and that was all that mattered. Maybe she should try dressing up a bit in the evenings. No use going around dressed like a man all her life.

Tossing the hat across the room, she turned away. Who was she fooling? He probably was delighted to get forty percent of her ranch just by standing up with her today. He'd be gone in a week to the life he loved, yet have the stability of her ranch behind him. Had she bargained away her home to a reckless traveling cowboy just to get over a rough spot in the road?

She refused to let the tears fall, though her throat ached. Lying in the dark, she counted the minutes, hours until Jase came in. She heard him walk down the hall, open the door to the room he'd used before. Close it behind him.

She heard the shower, the sudden silence when he shut it off. For one crazy moment she almost rose and went into his room, almost climbed into his bed just to see what he'd say to that.

But she couldn't risk it. Couldn't risk another slap in the face, another rejection. She closed her eyes as the tears seeped through her lids.

Shannon was flipping hotcakes when Jase entered the kitchen the next day.

"Good morning," she said easily, determined to give him no cause to suspect how much she wished last night had been different.

"Um, morning." He poured a large mug of coffee and took a hearty sip. Closing his eyes, he flicked them open to look at her warily.

"You're up early," he said.

"Sure. I wanted to check that bore near where the fire started. If we need to get it cleaned out, I want to assign a couple of the men to do it this week. Then I thought I'd swing by some of the fencing on the far end and see if it needs repair."

"One of the men could do that."

"I know, but I need the experience. Did Josh leave?"

"Yes. He could only stay a day. I spent the day before the wedding with him."

Relief he hadn't been having one last fling before they got married warred with a feeling of being excluded. He could have told her, could have had her meet Josh before the reception.

"Want to ride out with me?" Shannon asked as she sat opposite him. Both reached for the syrup at the same time. She nodded. "Go ahead."

He poured the warmed syrup over his stack of pancakes, then offered the container to her. Her fingers brushed his as she took it. Satisfied at the feeling that she still felt at his every touch, she began to eat.

"No. You can take Dink or someone with you if you

like. There's a lot to do here. I want to get the money transferred into your account. Make sure the feed store knows you have final word. Double check out a few of the schedules we devised. A week's not a long time."

"You think you'll be ready to go in a week?"

"I hope so. I've got the latest listing of the top contenders. I've mapped out the route I can take to get in as many stops as possible. If Shadow can hold up, we've got a long shot in the cutting events."

"How about bronc riding?"

He shrugged. "I don't know. I'll see how I do in the first few. Even if I can't catch up in the points, being in the money's at the local rodeo's good."

"I appreciate all you've taught me. I'm sorry you got hurt, but it's been a lifesaver for me. I'm grateful," Shannon said, wanting to say more, but unable to do so.

"Yeah, I know." There was no expression in his face or voice. He continued to eat.

The week flew by. Shannon tried to slow things down, tried to spend as much time as she could with Jase, but even the moments shared seemed to melt away.

And he kept busy. He spent hours every day working with Shadow, building up his endurance. He checked everything the men did, making sure each one knew his job, making sure each could manage with Shannon as boss. Made sure each one knew he'd be back.

The first thing Shannon noticed Thursday afternoon when Jase came in to dinner was the missing cast. Her heart stopped.

"It's off?" she said, staring, stunned. She hadn't even known he was going to town today. She'd been out near the river, and he'd never said a word.

"Off."

"How's your arm?" Slowly, as if pushing through molasses, she continued carrying the platter of ham to the table.

"Good as new. Ribs doing fine, too, the doctor said." He brushed past her to wash at the sink.

"So you'll be leaving soon, then." She placed the platter down carefully. As if any sudden motion would cause it to shatter. Disappointment and hurt settled in. She'd known it, why should she care now that the reality had arrived.

"In the morning," he said, his back toward her. It took a long time to wash his hands. "If I get started early enough I can make Kaycee in time for a two day event there."

"Then it's a good thing we're having ham tonight, it makes good sandwiches," she said, marveling that her voice continued to sound so normal. Inside she felt as if she were melting away. "Maybe I can make some cookies tonight for you to take."

"You don't have to bother."

"I don't mind."

When had he become so important to her? He was a part of her now. She could no more live without thinking of him than she could breathe. It went beyond the money he'd brought. While it helped, it only aided the ranch.

She needed him to complete something within

herself. The ranch meant nothing without him. She hoped he was still planning to come back. Hoped he told her the truth when he said he wanted to build up the place. To watch it grow from the ground up.

"Will you give me the schedule of rodeos you'll be competing in?" she asked as she poured their drinks. Her hands shook slightly. She tried to stop the shakes. She wouldn't make an idiot of herself. She had more pride than that.

"Yeah. I'll call you every couple of days to make sure you're all right." He sat down, his face closed.

"I'll be fine. I hope you get all the points you need to make the finals."

"You'll still come to Las Vegas?"

"I said I would."

They ate in silence.

When finished, Jase left to pack. Shannon baked cookies, cleaned the kitchen, packed a huge lunch. She felt numb the entire time.

It was late when she finished. Jase was still in the office. She paused in the door. "I packed you a lunch for tomorrow."

"Thanks. I'm leaving early. Sleep in. You don't have to get up when I leave."

"Okay."

He rose and came around the desk, his eyes on her. She watched until he reached the halfway point, then launched herself into his arms. Encircling his shoulders she held on tightly.

"Oh, Jase, don't go. I'll miss you so," she whispered, tears running down her cheeks.

His arms were like steel bands, molding her to him, pressing her tightly as if he'd never let her go.

"Darlin', you know I have to go. I've wanted this for so long. You knew I'd be leaving."

She nodded, clutching him tightly, breathing in the scent of him, imprinting the feel of him to never forget. She took a shaky breath, tried to brush away the tears before he saw them.

"I know. But you've done so much for me. Taught me so much, enabled me to hire the new men, buy the feed—"

"So help me, Shannon, if you mention how grateful you are one more time, I'll shake you."

She tried to smile. "I know. I am grateful, but I won't say it again."

"You take care of yourself," he said roughly.

"You, too. Don't go falling again." She didn't want to let go. She wanted to hold him forever.

"Don't worry about me, darlin', I'll be fine."

She nodded and turned her head, kissing his cheek. Then his mouth covered hers in a brief, searing kiss before he set her back, turned and gently shoved her out the door.

"I'll call."

She nodded and continued down the hall. Tears blurred her vision. He was leaving and there was nothing she could do but let him go.

Ten

The days dragged. But Shannon was not the same woman who had approached an injured rodeo cowboy several weeks ago. She had more confidence in dealing with ranch issues. She could direct the men, plan for the future. She knew enough about the computer program to continue to input historical data. Once things were running smoothly, she could use it for estimates of feed needs, lineages of the different stock, plan sales.

And if she needed help, she knew she could call on her neighbors, or ask Jase.

He called her the third night.

The call was not as satisfactory as she wished. He asked after the men, the stock, the horses. He'd even asked casually after her. But she wished he'd asked about her first.

She'd followed his progress on the schedule he'd left her. Asked how he'd performed. While she couldn't help wondering what he did between performances, she didn't ask. If he was out partying with the other cowboys she didn't want to know.

She refused to credit Jase with the same behavior as Bobby. He'd told her not to compare him to Bobby and she tried desperately not to. He was a different man and deserved to be respected for who he was.

Yet in the dark lonely nights, she wondered.

She missed him. The ranch didn't have the same obsession on her it once had. It became a place to live and to work. But without the person who made it all worthwhile, it just filled the time. She was restless, lonely.

She followed the professional rodeo website to follow the standings. The first couple of weeks she saw no mention of him. But then she saw he'd moved back into the top fifteen for cutting horses. A week later, he had enough points that he had a shot at the National Finals Rodeo after all.

She wondered if she dare take a few days and go see him perform.

Two weeks after his phone call, he hadn't called again. She went to bed each night wondering if she'd hear from him the next day, wondering if something was wrong. What if he'd tried to phone and she'd been out. If so, he'd neglected to leave a message.

She checked his itinerary before she went to bed. He was in Wyoming. It was a long way away. Out of sight, out of mind? She wanted him to call to tell her he was all right.

Shannon sat back in the office chair, vaguely pleased with the way things were going. The ranch was running smoothly. She was caught up on all the records, was confident in supervising the men and their tasks, and had easily handled the feed company when negotiating their latest order.

Her desk was clear. Feeling proud of her accomplishments, she glanced around, noting a stack of *Stockmen's Journals* waiting to be read. She hadn't had a chance since before Rod arrived at the ranch.

Since it had turned cool as October sped by, she was looking for something to do inside. She didn't want to go out in the late afternoon air. Might as well catch up on the reading. She reached for the most recent journal.

Curious, she flipped open the cover, leafed through. There was an article on—suddenly she stopped. There, facing her in full color, was a picture of Jase Hart. Her heart lurched as she studied the much loved face. What was his picture doing in the journal?

Scanning the article, she was stunned. Slowly she leaned back in the chair, began again, reading every single word.

"That lying, cheating, son of a bitch!" she hissed between clenched teeth, rereading the opening paragraph. "I'm going to find the meanest bronc in Texas and put him on it with his hands tied behind his back," she declared, surging to her feet and rummaging around on her desk until she found his itinerary. She was so mad she could spit!

"I'm going to stake him out on the plains and run a herd of cattle over him, twice!" She sought the date, matched it to where he was. Calculating how long it would take her to drive to Wyoming, she frowned and looked for where he'd be in two days.

She snatched up the journal again, still turned to the article. Seeing his picture had her plotting other dire actions she could take to make sure he understood just how angry she was. Who the hell did he think he was making a fool of her like that? She'd skin him alive!

It was late. Too late to leave today. She was not going to go haring off in the dark.

First thing tomorrow she'd be on the road. Oh, just wait until she caught up with him! She'd wring his neck.

Angry as never before, she flung the journal across the room, heard it hit the wall and fall with a plop to the floor. Pacing to control the fury that raged through her, she longed to face her husband, just for five minutes. She'd make sure he rued the day he'd lied to her.

She hadn't been this angry when Bobby had walked away. She hadn't felt this hurt in all the time she could remember.

"Just you wait, Jase Hart," she muttered, pacing the room.

Two and a half days later Shannon pulled her pickup truck into the fairgrounds holding the Trinity Rodeo. Pickups and horse trailers abounded, sharing the dirt parking lot with haphazardly parked cars. The area was designated for contestants. She had lied just a little to get in, but she figured it was justified. After all, it couldn't begin to match her lying husband.

She hopped out of the truck, turned to snatch up the rumpled journal, then slammed the door. Walking to the arena, she remembered the first day she'd met Jase. Anger boiled again. He could have said something that first day. Or any day since.

She stopped two cowboys. "I'm looking for Jase Hart, do you know him?"

"Know of him, rides broncs," one said, running his eyes over her trim figure, giving her a friendly grin.

"That's right, do you know where he is?"

"That event's going to go off in another few minutes, he's probably at the chutes," the other offered.

"And how do I get there?"

"You can't, unless you're a contestant. And the last I heard they don't take women."

Stalking away without a word, she bought a ticket for the stands. Climbing up until she had a good view of the arena, she found a seat in some shade and waited, quietly seething at the delay. The announcer was warming up the crowd. It was sparse; Friday afternoons were still working days for most folks. But the crowd was a respectable size. The stands would likely be full for tonight's show, and the Saturday ones.

Bareback bronc riding was the first event and she settled down to watch Jase compete. The first rider barely cleared the chute before falling. The second drew a horse that ran too mellow to rack up the points. The third rider scored in the low seventies. Jase was number four.

Shannon gripped her hands together as he began to ride. The horse went wild, bucking and corkscrewing, his unruly mane and tail flying in the wind. Jase raked his spurs on the shoulders, one hand held high, the other holding the rope. His hat jammed on his head, he concentrated on the ride.

Head almost between his knees, the horse tried to

dislodge the rider. His hind legs flew straight up. He swapped ends. All four legs hit the ground at the same time, jarring the rider. Jase held on. Eight seconds ticked by as if in slow motion.

Shannon held her breath, fear licking through her every single one of those endless seconds. Fear that he'd be bucked off, end up in the dirt again, maybe more injured this time than the last time.

She could scarcely stand it. Adrenaline poured through her as she willed him to stay on the horse, to stick to the saddle, finish the ride and get safely off. Her palms were slick, she rubbed them on her jeans. She couldn't stand it if anything happened to him. He had to finish the ride!

When the bell rang, she sagged back in the bench, relief flooding. He'd made it. In another couple of seconds the pickup men had him safely on the ground waving at the crowd. His score beat the next highest by two points.

Shannon scrambled out of the bleachers, heading toward the end of the chutes, no longer interested in the event. Thankful that he was safe, she still had something to say to her husband.

"Jase!" She found him at the end of the arena, laughing and joking with a bunch of other cowboys. They all looked the same, tall, rangy, dressed in blue jeans and colorful shirts. Their hats ranged from black to straw to snowy white. Most of them were younger than Jase. All of them swung around at the sound of Shannon's voice.

"Shannon?" He pushed away from the side of the

barn and headed toward her, his lopsided smile slowly forming. "What the hell are you doing here, darlin'? I've called you three nights running and got no answer."

"She yours?" one of the men asked.

"Yeah, she's my wife." It was said with quiet pride.

Shannon glanced at him, peered around at the group of grinning cowboys.

"No wonder you never chat up the girls, I wouldn't either if I had someone like her at home," someone else called.

"Something wrong at home?" Jase asked, taking her arm and turning her away from the rowdy cowboys. He walked her across the fairgrounds and toward the familiar truck and horse trailer. Shadow was tied in the shade, dozing.

"Nothing wrong at *my* ranch," she said firmly. Slapping him in the chest with the side of the journal, she stopped and glared at him, ignoring the small dart of pleasure that she felt seeing him. Trying her best to ignore how tanned he looked, how happy, how relieved she was that he'd finished the ride safely. Her anger flared again, hot and strong.

"But I wouldn't know about the Rafter C. Maybe you have more information than I," she snapped.

He looked at her, at the journal. Slowly he peeled it from his chest, lifting her fingers to release it. With a wary glance at her, he opened it. It took him only a second to find the article.

"Something you forgot to tell me?" she asked, eyes narrowed. "Like that first day in Fort Worth at the hospital? I thought you didn't have any place to stay while you recuperated. You never denied it."

"I never said I didn't, either," he answered carefully.

"You lied."

"No."

"The whole thing's been a lie from start to finish, hasn't it? You own the Rafter C. One of the largest and most successful ranches in Texas. God, you must have laughed yourself sick at my offering you a place to stay on the Bar Seven. How could I have been such an idiot?"

"Shannon—"

"You didn't need to stay at my place, you could have gone home and recuperated. Probably had a private jet fly out for you. Dammit, Jase, you lied the whole time!"

"No." He took her shoulders and shook her slightly to stop her tirade.

"Listen to me, darlin'. I was intrigued by your request. I knew I couldn't ride for a while so thought I might as well help you out. I remembered Bobby. He and I had been friends of a sort on the circuit. And I—"

She broke free and stormed away, turning after a dozen steps to stomp back. "All the time I called you irresponsible and you never said a word. According to that article you built that ranch up from a small, almost-bankrupt spread to a showplace. The brightest star in Texas ranching," she spat out. It had taken a lot more than a sense of responsibility to build up a huge ranch. It had taken hard work, grim determination and skill. Had he turned his back on it, shunned all duty since?

No, that didn't match with what she knew of him. He talked a good line, but responsibility was never far from him.

"Shannon, I'm trying to explain, if you would shut up for a minute."

"I'm so angry I could hit you!" she yelled, emotions churning. She felt anger, but also betrayal and hurt. She had fallen in love with a man who hadn't even done her the courtesy of telling her the truth about himself!

No! She would not let herself be in love with anyone. She would not! She would stand on her own two feet and guard her heart from hurt.

"Nobody's going to hit anybody. Calm down, dammit. I can explain. Just listen, okay? Everything I told you is true. I just didn't tell you everything there is to know."

The anger deflated.

Stunned as she realized she loved him, the anger faded. That was the reason she'd come, to see him again, to be with him. That's why the fear had been so strong when he rode, fear for the man she loved. Fear he might be hurt again.

She shivered at the thought of loving a man who would never be home, who wanted an irresponsible existence.

What she felt for Jase couldn't compare with what she'd ever felt before. How could she stand it? She leaned back against the side of the truck and gazed off across the fields. Her heart ached. In the distance she could see the wooden buildings of downtown Trinity silhouetted against the afternoon sky. It was hot. She didn't expect Wyoming to be so hot. It was already late October.

At home the trees had begun to turn and the nights

were cold. And she stood there beside her husband, a stranger she knew even less about now than she thought she had before. Knowing she loved him scared her more than anything.

She'd tried that once with a rodeo cowboy and failed. The hurt still lingered. But the fear of further hurt, deeper pain, was almost overwhelming. She couldn't love him.

"Why didn't you tell me?" she asked, the fight seeping out of her.

"For a number of reasons. None of them seem any good right at the moment. But at the time, I don't know, you didn't seem to know who I was and that was a novelty. I've had women come on to me because I own part of the Rafter C, or because I'm winning in rodeos or just because they think I have money. Not because they really want to get to know me."

"For money?" Funny, she'd taken his money, too. Didn't that make her like the others?

"That and the prestige. I thought I'd help you out while my arm healed, then move on. I hadn't expected it to turn out this way."

"Marriage, you mean?"

"Yes, that's what I mean." He ran his hand around the back of his neck, glancing down at the article. "They did the interview a few months back. They always do interviews months before they're published. To tell the truth, I'd forgotten about it."

"It's a very enlightening article. I should be even more reassured you know your stuff. No wonder I learned so much. Sorry for the shots about irresponsibility."

She closed her eyes. *Sorry I fell in love.*

"You made me so mad at first, equating me with Bobby. But then I guess I never gave you any reason to think differently," he said slowly.

"You still run it, don't you, even doing the rodeos." How could she have ever thought he was a man who shunned responsibility?

"No, Josh's managing it now. We talk from time to time, but he's in charge."

The anger that had driven her over 900 miles vanished. She felt drained, tired, depressed. What had she expected, for Jase to deny the article? Tell her a fairy tale that would make everything come out the way she wanted? Had she really pursued him, just to see him again, to gain some sort of reassurance that he would continue in their marriage, that one day he'd be back at the Bar Seven? The truth was she loved him and didn't like being parted, she wanted him home.

In truth she'd used the article as an excuse to see him again. The last weeks had been so lonely without him.

Love should bring happiness, joy. She felt almost sick. She wasn't sure, wasn't sure at all. All she knew was that it had been a mistake. From beginning to end, a huge mistake. And she was the one going to pay the price for it. If she could only undo the past, she'd make so many changes.

Not falling for a cowboy would be at the top of her list.

"I don't know why you wanted forty percent of my

operation. It can't amount to a hill of beans in comparison to what you already have." She rubbed her chest slowly, trying to ease the ache that was building.

"What you have, too, now, darlin'," he reminded her, watching her closely.

"What?" She looked at him.

"You have forty percent of my share of the Rafter C."

"I don't want your ranch." Good gracious, she'd never thought about that.

He smiled. "I know, but that was our agreement. I got forty percent of what you had and you got forty percent of what I had."

"But I thought you only had Shadow." She was dumbfounded. She had never considered this angle. "This changes everything."

Had he considered when they married that she'd own a part of his ranch? He must have.

She couldn't think.

Why would he have bargained away part of such a successful spread? And all in exchange for an almost-bankrupt ranch that would take years to turn around.

"It changes nothing. We're married. We'll remain married, make the most of it. How long are you going to stay?" Jase asked, rolling up the magazine, tapping it softly against his thigh.

"Huh?" She needed time to absorb all this.

"How long are you staying here?"

"I don't know." She rubbed her eyes. She was so tired. It had been a long drive down, and now she had to turn around and go all the way back. "I didn't plan on anything after seeing you. I was just so mad when I saw the article."

"Stay a few days, watch me ride," he said softly.

"What's the point?"

He drew her away from the truck, into his arms. Tightening them gently around her, he rested his head on her soft hair. "The point is to give your husband moral support while he challenges all comers."

"How are you doing?" His heat slowly invaded her body, softening her, warming her, exciting her.

"Luck's with me so far. I've earned enough money to gain the number fifteen spot in bareback bronc standings. Still below in the saddle bronc rides. And we're pulling in the points on the cutting events. Shadow's won seven in a row now. I've been in the money in most of the bronc competitions. But I'm not sure I'm going to make the finals in that one. There're others that are better than me. Just depends on how well I ride."

"And your ribs and arm?" she asked, slowly bringing her own arms up around his waist, leaning against the solid strength of him. Closing her eyes and breathing in his special scent brought her more alive than she'd been in weeks.

"Ah, I love your wifely concern. I'm doing fine, darlin'. Plan to stay a few days, the ranch'll manage just fine with the men you have working for you."

She hesitated.

"Come on, Shannon, at least until Sunday. I'm pulling out right after the show to head to Del Rio. You can stay here that long, watch me ride, watch Shadow and me compete. We'll go to some of the parties."

She shrugged. She didn't really like rodeos. She felt out of place, not having grown up around ranches like most of the participants.

And she didn't look forward to watching him ride. Rodeoing was a dangerous sport. The next time an injury could be more severe than a mere broken arm.

But she'd stay, just to have a few days with Jase. A few crumbs were better than nothing. She leaned against him, relishing the fleeting illusion of closeness.

"Good ride, Hart," a man called.

Jase nodded and waved, releasing Shannon.

"Come on, I'm hungry."

"It's mid afternoon," she protested.

"I know, but I don't eat before an event. So I'm ready now."

"What's the matter, nerves?" She turned and walked with him toward one of the numerous refreshment booths.

"Yeah. I'm afraid I'll toss my cookies if I eat before an event."

She smiled, charmed at the notion of her arrogant husband being nervous about anything. His arm lay heavy on her shoulder. He held her close, as if wanting the contact, or as if proclaiming to everyone that she belonged to him. Some of her hurt and fear faded in light of his obvious happiness in seeing her.

For a moment she let herself imagine he loved her.

She watched him compete in the evening show, wondering if she should subject herself to such terror. Every second seemed like an eternity. The horse he drew seemed meaner and more vicious than the one she'd seen earlier. Yet she yelled with the other fans and greeted him with a big smile when he joined her in the stands to watch the rest of the events. She'd never let him know how scared she'd been lest he suspect the deeper emotion behind it.

They attended the cowboys' dance afterward. Shannon met Jase's friends. For the most part they were men of his age, which surprised her. Jase didn't mingle much with the brash younger riders. His friends were ranchers and businessmen who loved rodeos, who competed on the local level but didn't follow the circuit.

From the comments made, Shannon realized this was the first dance Jase had attended since she'd met him. At least she didn't have the humiliation of knowing he saw other women when he wasn't with her. For that she was grateful.

It was late when Jase drove them to the motel near the fairgrounds where he had a room. Without asking, he got her one of her own. He kissed her cheek when he opened the door for her, dropping her suitcase inside.

"Breakfast at nine suit you?" he asked as he made to leave.

"When's your first ride?" she asked, not wanting him to leave, not knowing how to get him to stay.

"The bronc event starts at one. Shadow and I have an eleven-fifteen cutting event. We can get lunch after the bronc ride."

She nodded, reaching out her hand and trailing her fingers down his chest. She didn't want him to go.

He caught her hand and lifted it to his mouth,

planting a moist kiss in her palm. Folding her fingers over it, he released her and spun away. In seconds he hastened up the stairs to the floor where his room was situated.

Shannon shut her door carefully, longing to slam it, but was too conscious of other guests who were probably already asleep. Nothing had changed, she saw. Could she possibly work up enough nerve to let her husband know she didn't offer to sleep with him for gratitude?

And if he asked why she wanted to, what would she say? Dare she confess she loved him? Could she open herself up so much knowing he'd only married her to help her with the ranch?

Saturday repeated Friday, with more fans in the stands, more contestants, more action. The heat continued, the smell of dirt and horses and cattle permeated the fairgrounds. The loud roar when contestants scored high echoed around and around the stands. Jase scored in the top during the afternoon, second in the evening show.

When he drove them back from dinner to the dance on the fairgrounds, it was already close to midnight.

"Sure you want to go?" he asked as he cut the engine.

"Don't you? Bobby always liked the parties after the shows."

"Shannon, do me a favor and stop talking about Bobby Blackstone. He's dead and gone. And stop comparing me to him. We only had competing in common as I've come to discover. I don't want our marriage to be a threesome, you, me and Bobby."

"I'm sorry." She had been comparing them from the first and it wasn't fair to Jase. The more she was around him, the less like Bobby she found him. He had a strength Bobby never had, a concern for others she'd never seen with her first husband.

"For the record, I'm not like him."

"I know. It's just so hard to—"

"To what, let go of the past? Darlin', you've had some bad experiences, but all men are not like your first husband, nor your dad, and especially not like Rod Thompson. Give me a chance."

She nodded.

She loved him no matter what. If only she could express that so he'd see. But he'd see it as gratitude. And she was too uncertain to express her love. How would he respond?

He came around to open the door for her. Shannon swung her legs around and paused, reaching out to touch Jase's shoulder. "Jase?"

"Yeah?"

She swallowed. The darkness made it easier, nothing made it easy. "I, uh, wonder if you'd kiss me again? You haven't in a long time."

He became as still as a rock, trying to determine her expression in the faint light of the stars.

"Why?" A cold, hard word.

"I thought you liked to kiss me." Had she been wrong? Embarrassment rushed through her like wildfire.

"I do. I want to kiss you all the time. I'm afraid if I start I'll never stop." He pulled her from the cab, molding her slim body against his. One hand threaded beneath her braid, gently encircling her nape, the other around her slim waist.

Lowering his head, he kissed her, his lips firm and warm, his breath mingling with hers until they both forgot to breathe.

She reveled in the erotic sensations that bubbled up deep inside. She pressed herself against him wanting more, much more. Wanting to express her love physically while imagining he loved her in return.

His hand slowly came around to run down her side, moving to cup one breast, massage it gently, his thumb tracing the tight point of her nipple. His mouth left hers to trace soft kisses across her cheeks, down her throat, nuzzling the pulse point, tasting her. His lips were warm, his tongue like a brand against her soft skin.

"I don't want to start something we can't finish, darlin'. The first time we make love I want it to last as long as we want." His hand continued its sweet caress over the shirt and bra, continued to tantalize her breast.

"I want to taste every inch of you, from your sweet lips to your tiny toes." His hand moved down across the slight swell of her belly, the fiery waves of enchantment building as her skin became sensitized through the layers of her clothes.

"I want to bury myself in you and stay with you for days." His hand cupped her bottom and he pulled her tightly against him, demonstrating graphically how much he desired her.

"Tonight—" she breathed.

"No, darlin', the time's not right. I'm still not sure

186 | Barbara McMahon

your reasons are right, either. But I can wait. I told you, I want you for days on end, not a quick night when I have to get up to compete tomorrow.

The rodeo. Her heart sank. The rodeo always came first.

Her body was on fire and she wanted him more than anything. But the timing wasn't right. So just when would the timing be right?

"Hey, you two, break it up. You coming to the dance?" A half-drunk cowboy stumbled by, leering at them.

"Yeah." Jase eased away, swung an arm around her shoulders and led them into the dance.

Shannon refused to let his rejection drag her down. Time enough to think about it on the long drive home. Nothing had changed.

He said he wanted her, but she no longer believed him. He'd had more than one chance to make love with her and he continued to avoid it.

She raised her head and pasted a bright smile on her face, trying to ignore the longing that wouldn't ease. She'd pretend she was having a wonderful time tonight and leave at first light.

Jase had decided he'd prefer the rodeo, she'd accommodate him. Time to be heading for home.

Shannon didn't know if it was torture or the most exquisite pleasure to dance with her husband. Her body brushed against him, tingling and shivering in wild yearning. She could feel his heartbeat beneath her fingers, feel the strength and heat of his big body as they moved easily to the slow music. Pretending everything was fine between them, pretending they would go home together when it was over, was the closest Shannon came to fooling herself. She'd take the one night, one last dance and hold no regrets.

But when he dropped her by her room, she held his hand a moment longer than she should.

"Go to bed, darlin'." He brushed a sweet kiss across her forehead and turned away. "I'll see you in the morning."

She watched until he climbed the stairs. Resolutely she turned into the room and began packing. She wouldn't stay to watch him compete, it was too agonizing. She feared he'd be hurt again and she couldn't bear to see it. Anyway, he planned to leave right after the afternoon show. It couldn't matter to him if she left in the morning.

She had an idea she explored as she drove home. Thanksgiving was less than a month away. She'd throw out all the stops, invite his family, have the most lavish spread possible and convince him being at home was infinitely better than following the rodeos.

And she'd find the time he wanted if she had to give every ranch hand the week off with pay. If that was his only excuse, she'd make sure it was invalid. Somehow she had to convince her husband she wanted him as much if not more than he wanted her, all without revealing that she loved him.

It might be easier to compete with another woman than the draw of the rodeo, but she'd give it her best shot. Jase Hart was in for a surprise when he came home for Thanksgiving!

She swallowed hard. At least she hoped she could pull it off.

Eleven

"What the sweet hell were you doing leaving so blasted early Sunday?" Jase's voice growled in her ear when she answered the phone.

Shannon had been home six hours and was just sitting down to soup and a sandwich when the phone rang. Her heart skidded against her chest. Sighing softly, she sat on the edge of the desk, closing her eyes to see him better. Longings so severe they threatened to choke her swept through her at the sound of his voice.

"I had things to do."

"So important you couldn't even tell me you were leaving early?"

That had been pure cowardice. She couldn't tell him that.

"I'm waiting, Shannon." The anger in his tone rolled through loud and clear.

Glad for the distance, she scrambled around for an answer that would appease him yet keep her own vulnerability around him intact. "I have certain responsibilities—"

"And one of them is leaving without a word?" He swore softly.

"I'm sorry, Jase, you're right, that was wrong. I should have left a note or something."

"You should have waited until I got up and told me face-to-face, that's what you should have done. Don't give me any bull about responsibilities. Was there an emergency on the ranch?"

She almost lied, but he could so easily find out the truth.

"I just had to leave, okay? I'm sorry I didn't tell you first. How did you do on Sunday?"

"I won. Dammit, Shannon, you drive me nuts. You and I are going to have a serious talk when I get home. This isn't the end of it, Shannon."

"At Thanksgiving?" Would he come home before that? She held her breath.

"Right. See you then." The phone slammed down on the hook.

She slowly replaced her receiver, counting the days until Thanksgiving. If he had wanted, he could have found some time to stop by before then.

If he wanted.

Shannon was on edge. No doubt about it, she was plain scared. She'd planned for weeks now and as the time drew near she had butterflies the size of horses dancing in her stomach. Uncertainty was a constant companion. That and her longing for Jase.

She'd cleaned the house until it shone. She'd updated the two spare rooms for Brianna and Josh, pleased with the results. Of course, that placed Jase squarely with her.

Now she only had to convince her husband to share her room while his siblings visited.

She swallowed hard as she tried to envision his reaction.

Would he be happy with the decision? Or still coldly furious, thinking she only wanted him for gratitude. Men could be so dense sometimes.

Debating whether to invite Brianna and Josh for a long weekend, or plan to have them leave immediately after Thanksgiving dinner had given Shannon fits. In the end she opted for the extended weekend. If things didn't work out as she hoped with Jase, she'd have them as a buffer.

Would Jase himself stay beyond Thursday? Or would she end up entertaining his family while he hit the circuit again? She wished she knew what he was doing. What he was thinking.

Where he was!

Sighing softly as she arranged late fall flowers on the dining room table, she hoped everything went smoothly this weekend. Brianna was arriving today. Josh tomorrow around one, Thanksgiving afternoon.

When Jase would show up was anyone's guess.

He hadn't phoned her since that one call after she returned from Trinity. Their relationship had definitely cooled, not that there was much of a relationship to cool with him hundreds of miles away.

She missed his calls, missed him totally. Wondered if he missed her a fraction as much as she missed him. Wondered if his dreams at night were of her as hers were of him.

He might be home today or tomorrow at the latest. He hadn't told her when to expect him, just that he'd be home for Thanksgiving.

She was counting on it. She was going to seduce him. She'd planned every move. Swallowing as the minutes ticked by, the time drawing closer when she'd have to put her plan into action, she rubbed her palms against her jeans.

She'd missed him like she'd never missed anyone before. She loved him more deeply than she'd ever imagined loving anyone. Whatever he wanted would be fine with her, as long as he treated her like his wife.

At the knock at the front door she knew her first guest had arrived. How long before Jase arrived?

An hour later Shannon had shown Brianna to her room and given her a brief tour around the house. Now they sat in the living room, sipping hot chocolate. Tall and blond like her brother, Brianna Hart displayed the same self-assurance he did. But on her it came across as confidence, not arrogance. Shannon liked her instantly.

"It's miserable out. The snow's coming down faster than my wiper blades could keep up," Brianna said as she sat across from Shannon, near the fire. "But I wouldn't have missed this for anything. I'm so glad to finally meet you. I was so astonished when Jase called to tell me he was getting married."

"It happened rather suddenly," Shannon murmured, not knowing what to say. Jase should be here. He should have welcomed his sister to his home.

"I'll say. But it's just like Jase. He always knows what he wants. And once he sets out to get something, watch out. He always gets it."

"Oh?" Shannon frowned. What had he really wanted by marrying her?

"Sure, like keeping us together when our folks died. Or making the Rafter C the best ranch in the state."

"You were lucky to have him," Shannon said, envying Jase's sister for the love she knew she had from her brother.

"Josh and I both know it. That's why we were so pleased when you didn't object to his competing. He's wanted this for so long. It was a dream from when he was a kid. Having to raise us almost put paid to that dream. We're so glad he's able to go after it."

"Competing in rodeos?"

"Yes. Funny, isn't it. I mean, after working at a ranch all the time you'd think the last thing a man would want to do is go play at rodeos. I prefer a nice restaurant and dancing. Or a movie."

Shannon nodded thoughtfully. "So he'd dreamed of this for ages." It wasn't just a whim, a shirking of responsibilities. It was a dream, a lifelong dream.

Things shifted slightly. Made more sense. He'd said it was something he'd wanted, but a lifelong dream? No wonder he was so adamant.

"Ever since he was a teenager. He competed in the junior rodeos around the ranch when Mom and Dad were alive. I thought he'd given up, but when I finished college Josh and I insisted he try it. He did well the last couple of years. I hope he makes the finals, he's getting up there, you know."

Shannon smiled, remembering when she'd

mentioned age how indignant he'd become. "He has a good shot at the cutting event. And an outside one for the bareback bronc riding."

"I know, we're following the rankings. I hope he wins one or the other." Brianna tilted her head as she studied Shannon. "Josh told me you were pretty. But he didn't tell me how tiny you are. I feel like a giant around you. How do you stand up to Jase?"

Shannon glanced up and met her smile. "I'm not so small I can't hold my own with your brother." The words echoed around and around in her head.

She stood toe-to-toe with him sometimes. But she never feared him. Only feared the overwhelming feelings she experienced around him.

"Josh said you'd have him wrapped around your little finger before Jase knew it."

Startled, Shannon stared at her. "Are you kidding me? Do you really think anyone can wrap Jase around anything?" The idea was mind boggling. Then she giggled softly. What a wonderful thing it would be, however far-fetched. Her heart lurched just thinking about him.

Brianna smiled and nodded. "I know, but that's what Josh said. When's Jase coming?"

"Today or tomorrow. I'm guessing tomorrow now that the weather's turned so bad."

"Good, then it's just us girls tonight. Tell me all about falling in love with my brother."

Shannon stared at her. How had she known? Or was she only guessing? Slowly, picking her words carefully, Shannon told Brianna about meeting Jase.

Later that night Shannon lay awake thinking over all she'd learned from Brianna. No wonder Jase put so much emphasis on the rodeo, it had been a lifelong dream of his, one that he was in danger of growing too old for before he had a chance to make his mark. She knew about lifelong dreams. Hadn't she had one for home and stability and family? Wasn't that what made her marriage so much harder to accept? She wanted more than Jase could give her.

Or she thought she had. Now she wasn't so sure. Maybe she'd take whatever time he could spare for her and enjoy it. Life wasn't perfect.

Instead of rejecting anything less than perfection, she needed to accept what she had and make the most of it. She wanted him with her always, but a few weeks at a time would be better than nothing.

From what Brianna had said, Shannon knew neither she nor Josh realized the full extent of all Jase had given up to raise them. He'd never told them, never burdened them with any guilt. Yet he'd shared that feeling of missing things with her. She felt closer to him than ever. If he could share private feelings with her, ones he'd never shared with anyone else, it augured well for their future. Now she had to make him see that, too.

She needed to let him know she wouldn't burden him with responsibility. She could take care of the ranch. If he would only come to see her from time to time, life would be so much richer than what she'd had the last few years. Richer by far than she'd ever known. She loved him. And that made life richer for her. Whatever he decided to do, it wouldn't take away the warmth loving him brought her.

The snow stopped during the night, the sky cleared, and Thanksgiving Day dawned bright and sunny. The pristine setting was picture perfect. Snow graced the bare limbs of the trees. Footprints showed clearly where the cowboys had walked to do the routine chores. They would celebrate in the bunkhouse. Shannon had reserved the house for family only.

She and Brianna worked well together in the kitchen as they prepared the traditional meal.

"This is great," Brianna said. "I love to fix all the trimmings and then watch my brothers eat it. They can put away a ton of food."

"I'm glad you're here. I never had anyone to prepare the meal with before. Mostly when my dad was alive, we ate at the base."

And Bobby had spent only one Thanksgiving with her, watching football while she worked alone in the kitchen.

The preparations continued through the morning. They basted the turkey regularly. The dressing was prepared. Sweet potatoes casserole made. Corn shucked and ready to be boiled. Biscuits started and set aside to pop into the oven when the pies were finished.

Shannon set the big dining room table. The entire house was redolent with the aromatic fragrance of the savory meal. Nibbling as they worked, neither gave thought to stopping for a full lunch. Dinner would be enough.

When a truck pulled into the driveway, Shannon looked up, butterflies in full dance. She brushed her hands across the apron she wore to protect the soft rose-colored skirt and sweater she'd put on in honor of the day.

Checking that her hair was still somewhat tidy, she ran her fingers through it. Should she have worn her braid today? No, pulled back to hang down her back made her appear more feminine. She refused to admit why that was so important today. But she hoped Jase liked it.

Peering out the kitchen window, she could just catch a glimpse of the familiar truck, the horse trailer.

"It's Jase, isn't it?" Brianna asked excitedly, looking out with Shannon.

"Yes."

"Shall I leave? I don't want to spoil his homecoming. If you're shy about kissing, I can step into my room for a few minutes."

Shannon whirled around, staring at her. Of course Brianna would expect a fervent homecoming, her husband of less than two months had been gone for weeks.

Would Jase kiss her?

"No, stay. He'll be happy to see you."

The minutes dragged. How long did it take to unload Shadow and give him some feed? Each second seemed like an eternity. Shannon stared at the door, her heart in her throat. Then she heard him knocking the snow off his boots against the porch step. Mesmerized, her eyes watched the knob, scarcely realizing when it turned.

He came in quickly, closing the cold behind him. He

wore a dark hat, a warm shearling coat and the usual jeans and boots. He looked good enough to eat.

"Hello, darlin'," he said. "Brie!" He strode across the room in three long strides and caught his sister up in a hug.

Then turned to Shannon, watching her warily for a moment before catching her tightly against him. He lowered his face to hers. He was cold, his cheeks, lips, nose icy against her flushed skin. But soon, soon the heat between them warmed him up, warmed her up. It felt so good to be held by him, to have his strong arms around her, his mouth moving against hers, his tongue seeking admittance. Her arms tightened and she held on. Time was forgotten. There was only the reality of Jase, home at last.

"A simple kiss on the cheek always did for me," Brianna said, laughing.

Jase drew back, his eyes still on Shannon, gazing deep into hers as if seeking the answer to a unspoken question.

"Yeah, but you're easily pleased," he said, slowly releasing his wife.

Brianna laughed again. "I like your wife."

"Me, too," Jase said, trailing his knuckles across Shannon's cheek. He turned and shrugged out of his heavy coat.

"Something sure smells good," he said, glancing warily at Shannon

"Dinner," she said breathlessly, unnecessarily, unable to take her eyes from him. "We plan to eat around six. Josh's supposed to be here about one."

She was still nervous. He'd come home, now the hard part, getting him to stay. To want to stay with her. She knew she'd have to share him with the rodeo. She'd accepted that, to keep his dream alive. But she wanted him to come back to her whenever the rodeo didn't call.

"I'll clean up and be right out," Jase said, heading toward the bedrooms. He wrapped one large hand around Shannon's upper arm and propelled her from the room. "You and I need to talk," he said grimly. "Make yourself at home, Brie," he called to his sister.

Glancing over her shoulder to see an amused Brianna watching them, Shannon stumbled at the pace Jase set.

He reached the door to the room he once used when Shannon pulled them to a stop.

"Jase! Brianna's using this room."

He stopped, turning her around until she stood before him. Her palms were damp, her lips dry, her heart thudded heavily in her chest.

"The other room?"

"I fixed it up for Josh."

"Where the hell am I supposed to stay?"

She swallowed hard. "In with me?"

Startled, his grip tightened. His eyes narrowed as he flicked a glance toward her room, back to her.

"I had to put you in with me. I gave Brianna the room you used to use and Josh has the other spare room and you can't stay in the bunkhouse."

"So we're sharing?" His voice carried no emotion. His expression was blank.

She nodded, biting her lower lip. This wasn't going

quite like she had hoped. The silence stretched out endlessly.

His hand came up to cup her chin, his thumb rubbed the lip. "Don't do that, you'll hurt yourself."

She began to tremble at his touch. Her hand grasped his wrist, held on. When his thumb brushed across her lips again and again, she thought her knees had melted. Breathing became difficult. Her whole being focused on Jase and his light touch on her lip.

"Why are we sharing, Shannon?" he asked softly, lifting his gaze from his thumb to lock with hers.

"I—it's what your brother and sister would expect. We're married," she explained, wondering where the courage she'd tried to pump up had fled.

He shook his head, his expression furious. "All for show?"

Slowly she shook her head, panic flooding her senses. The time for honesty was long past. "I want you to stay with me."

"Why?" It sounded like a shot.

She held his gaze, drawing on every bit of courage she could muster. "I want you as much as you want me." Her voice was strong, true, her eyes never wavered from his.

"Gratitude for helping at the ranch?" he snarled, his fingers biting into her jaw.

She shook her head slightly, her gaze never faltering. "No. Desire, pure and simple." She held her breath. There was more. "And wanting, needing, lust. Love. If you still want me." Her heart banged against her chest. Way to go, Shannon, she thought in disgust, so much for seduction.

He swooped and picked her up. In only seconds they were in her bedroom, the door slammed behind them. Jase pressed Shannon up against the cool wood, towering over her. His hand traced down the soft wool of her sweater, tracing her fine bones beneath her shoulder, running his fingers down one breast.

"I've wanted you since you walked into the cubicle in the emergency room last September," he said as his mouth consumed hers. His hunger fed hers and instantly they strained for a deeper closeness than either had ever known. His lips claimed, his tongue mated, his hands roamed over all of her body, igniting craving flames that threatened to consume her.

Easing back just a little, Jase cupped her face in his warm palms, tracing every inch of her flushed skin with his eyes. "You look pretty, Half Pint."

His hands drifted down her neck, to her shoulders, rubbing against the soft rosy sweater. When he raised the soft wool, his hands were gentle against the silky camisole beneath.

When he shrugged out of his shirt, she lightly touched the smooth skin that covered hard muscles, her fingertips brushing into the tangle of hair on his chest as she had longed to do that first day at the hospital.

He kissed her and the magic began.

Absorbed by him until they were one, she relished the sensations. Glowing lights, incredible heat, and overwhelming love, the sensations shimmered through her until that was all she could feel, all she could experience. Thought was impossible. Only Jase defined

REBEL HEART | 201

her existence.

When they reached the summit together, it was glorious. Time seemed to cease. The world faded. The only reality was Jase and Shannon, in a cloud of pure love.

"Tell me," he said urgently, lightly kissing her rosy lips. "Tell me about desire." Another kiss. "And wanting." Another kiss. Another. "And love."

A slow, deep kiss that was as gentle as the rain in the spring, as sweet as honey, as exciting as fireworks.

Her heart threatened to break from her chest. She could scarcely breathe. Every nerve ending overloaded with the electricity generated by Jase. The pure tactile responses were more overwhelming than anything she'd ever experienced.

"I like it when you touch me," she said shyly.

He laughed softly. "I like touching you. I need to touch you. When I do, I'm complete. When we're apart, I'm not. How did that happen? How did just being with you complete me when I thought I had my life in order before?" Jase's voice sounded soft, husky in her ear. His breath warmed her neck, her shoulder. His weight was like a heavy blanket on a cold night.

She'd never be cold again.

Her hair swirled around the pillow, some of it settling on her shoulder. He threaded his fingers in it and drew them through and through, combing the silky tresses with his hands. Then lifted his head to gaze down at her.

"Beautiful." Jase traced her lips with a finger tip. Shannon caught her breath.

"You were telling me about desire," he said, looking deep into her smoky eyes.

"You said you wanted me," she whispered, longings so strong she could scarcely stand them. His touch wreaked havoc with every nerve ending. The spiraling craving grew by leaps and bounds with every stroke of his fingertips. Surely she couldn't want him again so soon.

"I've wanted you from the first. I told you all along," he said. "It sure wasn't a secret."

"And you said I should let you know if I wanted you back," she stalled.

He smiled his lopsided smile, his eyes silvery in the dim light. "You let me know just fine, darlin'. Now tell me the part about love."

She hesitated.

"Come on, darlin', tell me." His hands captured her face again, his fingers threading gently into her soft hair.

"I love you, Jase," she said.

"Was that so hard? I love you, Shannon Hart. I have forever I think. At least from the day I met you." His kiss ignited a flame.

Shannon gave all she had to the embrace, reveling in the words that had exploded through her like a firecracker. Did he mean it? Could he really love her, only her?

When he ended the kiss, she held his head close to hers, not wanting to end the contact.

"You never said you loved me. Not when you asked me to marry you, or any other time."

"Are you kidding? It was all I could do to get you to

agree to a marriage without loading you up with guilt about loving you when you made it clear you didn't love me. What chance did I have with you thinking I was like a certain party that shall remain unnamed in our bed. You were all for staying as far from a man as you could get. All you wanted was to learn how to run your ranch."

"Well that was then. I hardly knew you," she tried to explain.

"When you were fighting that blasted fire I was so afraid you'd get hurt. That's when I knew I loved you. That I wanted to share your life. When the insurance money wasn't there, I saw a chance to get close enough to you to have a way to come back. I wasn't going to be just your partner. Yet all you seemed to feel was gratitude. I wanted to die when you offered yourself out of gratitude."

She traced a finger along his shoulder, watching as her fingertip registered the heat and strength of his muscles beneath his skin. She couldn't argue with him, she hadn't admitted she loved him then.

"But you have your dreams, too, and have to follow them," she said, hoping she understood. Hoping she wouldn't say anything to spoil this moment. Her heart almost exploded with happiness.

Jase loved her!

"Yeah. Can you understand?"

"I think so. Only, I don't think I like watching you when you compete. I'm too afraid you'll take another spill. Next time it might not be a broken arm but a broken head!" She remembered her fear as she'd watched him ride in Trinity.

"Nah, it'll never happen. But if I do, I have a place to recuperate." He nuzzled her neck, trailing kisses to the underside of her jaw.

"You had a place all along—the Rafter C." She sank further in love with him showing no sign of wanting to end their intimacy. His sister probably wondered if they were coming back out tonight.

"But you weren't there, only here. Darlin', when you walked into that hospital room, I was glad I was lying down or you'd have flattened me. I was intrigued by you from the start. And when you told me about your first husband, it hurt me to know you hurt. I wanted to change things for you, show you it didn't have to be like that."

"You could have corrected me when I started in comparing you two." Her hands roamed over him relishing every tantalizing touch.

After so many years alone, Shannon reveled in sharing with another. In being with Jase.

"I wanted you to want me no matter what. Even if you thought I was an irresponsible rodeo cowboy."

"And I did. I fell in love with you ages ago. Only after we were married, instead of drawing closer, we seemed to pull apart. I couldn't help remembering how it had been before." She rubbed her hands over the rippling muscles of his back, savoring the feel of his hard body against hers. Shannon knew she'd never feel alone again.

"I didn't want gratitude."

"That's not the reason I love you."

Yet she would always be grateful. Not only to him,

but to the fates that had brought them together. Her life had been incomplete before Jase. She knew now what he felt. Grinning, she looked up at him.

"So I make you complete, huh?" she asked, the deep pleasure at hearing his earlier words like a soothing balm to her scarred heart.

"From the beginning. I touch you to be connected. I can't keep my hands off you, in case you hadn't noticed. You're so soft and feminine, yet strong enough to face any challenge. It's a wonderful combination. One I want to share forever. That was the talk I planned to have with you...I was going to stop your foolishness and make this marriage real."

She smiled slowly. "You did. I was afraid you might not come home before Las Vegas, though you said you'd be here for Thanksgiving."

"Darlin', you had me so crazy I didn't know which end was up. I thought I wanted to forsake all responsibility for a while. But once I left here all I could do was wonder how you were, how the repairs were going, how the men were working out. I wanted to be a part of it all. Even winning the rodeo events doesn't mean as much as it did. Once the Nationals are over, I'm coming home for good."

"But I thought riding in the rodeos was your dream."

"It was and this year I've got as good a shot as I'll ever have at winning an event at the National Finals. But win or lose this season, I'm not going on the circuit again. It takes too much time away from you. I've got a new dream now."

She reached up and kissed him, her heart almost bursting with happiness. It was more than she ever expected.

"Of course we need to work on your timing," Jase said sometime later. "My sister probably figures she'll have dinner by herself."

"*My* timing! If you hadn't been so concerned about your ride the next day we could have had a fine night in Trinity. And I wanted to make this Thanksgiving special. It's the first one with my new family."

"And probably the smallest gathering we'll ever have." He kissed her one last time and slowly rolled over beside her, reluctant to be parted.

"What do you mean?" She sat up, knowing it was past time to get dressed. They had guests, a wonderful dinner to eat and blessings galore to be thankful for.

"I mean, next year at this time I expect a son or daughter to join us."

The gladness almost shattered her composure. "Oh, Jase, a baby? I'd love to have your baby."

"A father has a lot of responsibility, but I figure I'm up to it. You might say I'm experienced that way already." His voice held a wealth of satisfaction. "I love you, darlin'. How long did you say Brianna and Josh were staying?"

—The End—

I hope you enjoyed **Rebel Heart.** If so, would you be so kind as to leave a review at the vendor where you purchased it? Reviews can be long or short, they are always a help. Thank you.

Books in THE HARTS OF TEXAS Series

Rebel Heart (Book 1)

Tangled Hearts (Book 2)

Reckless Heart (Book 3)

Please visit my website: www.barbaramcmahon.com
for a complete list of all my books.